Dancing Naked

IRON PRESS
An Indie Publishing Cooperative
Ironpress101@gmail.com

All author's work contained within these pages are under individual copyright agreement. All rights reserved, digital or otherwise.

No part of this book may be reproduced in any written, electronic, recording, or photocopying without written permission of the publisher or author. The exception would be in the case of brief quotations embodied in the critical articles or reviews and pages where permission is specifically granted by the publisher or author.

Although every precaution has been taken to verify the accuracy of the information contained herein, the author and publisher assume no responsibility for any errors or omissions. No liability is assumed for damages that may result from the use of information contained within.

Cover Design: Toby Kalman
Editor: Arthur Clark
Setup: Dwight Ritter, Toby Kalman, Geri Rider, Sharon Anderson

Print: ISBN 978-0-9909672-3-1

E-Book: ISBN 978-0-9909672-4-8

"Dancing is nothing more than making love set to music."

-Anonymous

PREFACE

We hope you enjoy this anthology of short stories and poems compiled by the Osterville Writers Group. Within these pages you will find the naked souls of each of the authors dancing across the pages, creating pictures with the words they write.

As an anthology, the stories stand alone for your perusal, not dropped into any category or genre, but offered as a piece of each and every one of the author's personal life's journey.

This group dates back several decades to the Ten O'Clock Scholars and an early member instrumental in founding the Cape Cod Writers Center to which we are still affiliated.

The current members are as diverse as the weather on the Cape. We have die-hard pragmatists and free spirits with a few rag tag moderates to soothe egos and minimize bloodshed. Despite our different styles, our critique sessions affirm our belief in each other's writing and move us forward in our craft.

In the midst of the winter doldrums, one creative member challenged the rest of us to write pieces that could be incorporated in a book with a publication date of mid-summer. Despite not being under the influence of any mind-altering substances, we all agreed that this was a great idea.

Since we were in the midst of one of the worst winters in Massachusetts history, our outlook wasn't all that cheery, meaning that the common themes running through the stories reveal the naked truth that life isn't all sunshine and thornless roses.

Whatever the motivation, this anthology is the result of our group effort to produce and publish quality writing that will entertain and perhaps challenge the reader to thoughtfully consider our topics.

ACKNOWLEDGEMENTS

No book is ever completed without the aid and assistance of many people for whom we give our eternal gratitude and thanks.

First, for the Cape Cod Writers Center. Without this organization, we would not have come into being.

Second, The Osterville Methodist Church for the blessed use of their parlor each week on a Tuesday morning where our creativity and camaraderie come to life.

Next, to our wonderful families for their patience, encouragement and, at times, their blatant criticism, more than likely justly deserved, and for which we are grateful. (They make us better writers.)

To Toby for her beautiful painting for the cover of this book. For Dave and Michael at Country Press who accept our manuscripts and magically turn them into real live books.

And special thanks for the Osterville Writers Group, and their support, editing and unconditional love and acceptance of what we write, but more importantly, for who we really are.

No offense meant for any omissions.

Dancing Naked

An Anthology

CONTENTS

ROBERT BUYER *Mathematics*	*1*
ARTHUR F. CLARK *Blood Lines*	*3*
DWIGHT RITTER *The Secret*	*19*
TOBY KALMAN *The Gift*	*37*
MIKE TEMPESTA *Salvation Soll*	*43*
DWIGHT RITTER *Smackwater Jack*	*59*
SHARON ANDERSON *The Crystal Chronicles*	*67*
MIKE TEMPESTA *Eleanor*	*75*
WADE SAYER *Rogue Radio*	*131*
WADE SAYER *When Sammy Came Home*	*143*
TOBY KALMAN *Moving Images*	*151*
TOBY KALMAN *Jo-Henry's Day*	*153*
GERI RIDER *Retribution*	*185*
ARTHUR F. CLARK *Sitting Ducks*	*193*
ROBERT BUYER *The Living Sea*	*213*
ROBERT BUYER *Mending Nets*	*217*
SHARON ANDERSON *Angelic Intervention*	*219*
TOBY KALMAN *Fields*	*227*
GERI RIDER *A Mother's Gift*	*233*
SHARON ANDERSON *Emily*	*235*

DANCING NAKED

MATHEMATICS

Numbers are constant
No one can deny.
One plus one is always two.
Super computers cannot dispute.
Empirical facts are deficient.
Behold the Eastern Cottontail.
For millenniums they have shown
That one plus one makes multitudes.

DANCING NAKED

DANCING NAKED

BLOOD LINES

"You fucking little piss-ant nigger! I can't figure why you was ever born, but I guess we'll take care of that dumb-ass mistake right now!"

A muddy, booted-foot followed by a grunt from the energy put into it lifted the youth half-off the faded linoleum floor. Landing in a fetal position, the boy instinctively hunched his shoulders to protect his head. The ongoing beating was sadistic and brutal. Welts and tears reflected the places on the young man's bare torso where each kick and blow landed. Included was detail down to the imprint of the man's upscale hunting-boot's coarse tread.

Blood was splattered across the floor in whatever direction the assailant's shod foot had taken it. Further up, a smear on the wall marked where the first, ham-handed fist broke Jake's nose and took him down. The calcimined tin-ceiling caught its share too. The lad's hair swiped it like a paint-brush as he was picked up bodily then slammed back to the floor.

Winded from the effort, and assuming his mission complete, the bulky intruder rattled around in the kitchen for a few minutes. Headed out through the door, the man stomped at the boy's head one last time as he walked past, the screen door slapping shut in his wake.

Barely fourteen years old, Jake was groggy but still had his wits about him. In agony, he dared not move for fear his tormentor might be looking, but then began to wonder if he could. He figured it was five minutes that he lay there, but it may have been two or twenty. None-the-less, it took a monumental act of self-control.

*

His parents, locked by circumstance into being dirt poor farmers, and down on their luck, the boy carried visions of somehow breaking out of what was basically indentured servitude. Called sharecropping, he understood the term only too well. In his mind it was a mockery. The true meaning: another white man's word for legalized slavery.

Jake had been scrawny as a child, but now he was filling out. A good boy, he was dutiful and smart, and his mother saw that he never missed a day with his lessons. Also noting his dedication and basic quickness of mind, Missy Hills, his teacher at the all black school, seemed to take a special interest in the young man. She said the boy had spirit, and unlike most of his classmates, had the desire to succeed. Amongst her thirty-odd students of all grades, he alone displayed a hunger to learn. The woman did her best to steer him to levels well in advance of his age.

Of mixed race, the only Negro blood came from his grandmother. With her blue eyes, blondish wavy hair, and light complexion, those who cared or kept track of such things had to admit any racial overtones had faded to a meaningless blur.

Yet, some knew. Knew and remembered.

The year was 1918 when the land-owner's father had gotten Jake's grandma pregnant. Legally, that meant Jake's mother, Edie May, was a half-sister to the man who now owned the land. A relationship a Southern white man of means could never admit to, and the obvious reason the boy's family had been mostly ignored. As poor cousins, they were kept close, out of sight, poverty-stricken, and the past a secret buried so deep it was hoped its memory would rot like last year's squash, and the remnants plowed under.

The Korean War was winding down, and there were rumors the boss-man wanted to run for public office. Known as a bully in his youth, he grew up in military academies, and graduated from a college noted for its similar structured bearing. He spent WWII as a Captain in a local Army Reserve unit. There, he offered asylum to the draft eligible sons of those whose friendship he wished to cultivate. When the War ended, the man was well-connected, both socially and politically to those in power. His hand in a number of State and County Commissions, most would think he was a shoo-in, but in this part of the south, memories were long. It would be extremely difficult to win an election with that stain of tainted blood in the family.

Proud and brave as any other American, men of color served and died for their country, no matter they did so without a voice. To keep it that way, there were Secret Societies that had been around since the Civil War ended. Formed to intimidate, and keep former slaves, the poor, and the ignorant in check, Jake's uncle was rumored to be the current leader of the local den. Members-only meetings were held often, with bonfires that lit the country-side. Silhouettes of hooded figures could be seen against the flames, performing their ritual ceremonies. No one questioned their meaning or intent, for everyone knew. Once in a while there'd be a lynching. Trumped up charges, or insult, it mattered little why. The true reason: to keep certain people in their place, and put fear in the hearts of those who remained. Blacks walked quietly, eyes cast downward, and stepped to the gutter when white folk passed on the sidewalk.

Tragic accident was no stranger to Jake's family. The boy's older brother had been killed by a never-caught, hit-and-run driver. His sister was found dead soon after. Apparently she'd drowned in a nearby, knee-deep creek. Her head bloodied from where she'd fallen on a rock along the stream's edge. The Police seemed more inclined to stamp "Death by Accident" on such case files rather than investigate. Coincidentally, one of their senior Commissioners was also known as the Grand Giant of the Province.

Not everything was a downer in Jake's life. There was his cousin, Mary Lu. Bright-eyed and beautiful, she and the boy had often played together until their mutual grandpa died. The old man was always referred to as a good person by anyone Jake knew, despite never fully accepting half the fruit of his loins. The family Patriarch, he'd passed on his blue eyes and blond hair to Jake's mother. Edie May graduated high-school in '36, in the midst of the depression. Facing little hope for work, the old man sent her off to a secretarial school in DC.

Lonely and heart-sick for her piney-wooded Carolina, she met a boy her own age who was newly arrived from Germany. Raised on a farm, his parents had rushed him out of Europe when Hitler began rattling swords, and laying the ground work for his Third Reich.

Gunter had been sponsored by his uncle, and was living with him in Maryland while he sought work. The young man was as lonely as Jake's mother, alienated from the only world he knew, and tired of standing in bread lines. Edie May worked in a welfare office as part of her training. There, she helped applicants fill out forms. With his sad eyes, broken English, and bashful ways, the girl fell for him like a child for a new puppy. This was not love at first sight so much as a mutual need for each other. They fit like pieces in a puzzle. Only a month had gone by when the girl wrote to her mother, and begged her to break the news to her father and benefactor. She wanted to quit school, get married, and come home to a life on the farm. Troubled by his secret love for an earthy, mixed-breed, the old man could not deny the child such a simple request. To ensure the girl's future, he drew up legal papers that stated she would always have a place on his sizeable holdings, and be provided with work, food, and housing.

Jake's grandma must have really loved that old man, and he her. For years, when his sickly missus was away, or in the hospital, grandma would go up to the main house to clean for him and cook his meals. Gram never said a word, good or bad about these visits, but she would be smiling and happy for days afterward.

Jake somehow understood the relationship.

*

Everything changed in the dark days after grandpa's death. Mary Lu was sent to an uppity, academically-noted, out-of-town school. To add to her misery, the girl's father told her she was to have nothing more to do with niggerly poor folk, like Jake.

While dealing with her own sorrow, Jake's grandmother watched the boy too slip into a state of melancholy. Weather permitting, the old lady spent most days in her rocker on the front porch. Today she tugged at Jake's shirt as he passed. He turned and went down on one knee so he'd be on her level, and close enough to understand her raspy whisper. "Dat uncle of yours, don't mind him, boy. He don't know much about nothin'. If Mary

DANCING NAKED

Lu was meant to be, she was meant to be. How a man so lovin' as your Grampa could produce both good and bad seeds, I'll never know. Your Momma, she's a good woman. Always has been. Your uncle, on the other hand, was born with the colic, and turned mean and ugly right from the start. Well, boy, nothin' lasts forever. The times they is a changin', and he just don't know it yet."

Not fully understanding the message his Grandmother had labored to tell him, Jake kissed her forehead and went about his business. The old lady died a few weeks later.

Her lover's resting place was the family crypt on the highest point of land in the family's holdings. Gram was put in the ancient slave plot, as close to the old man as they could get her.

Quite taken with Jake's brightness and work ethic, and certain it would be for naught if left untended, his teacher approached the boy's mother. Aware of the family's financial status, Missy Hills suggested she'd try to open some doors for him.

With his mother's permission, the woman worked her way through various levels of government bureaucracy with little luck. That is until in recopying the boy's application over and over, inadvertently entered, German, where the form asked for race. Evidently that was close enough to Caucasian for whoever read the form, and Jake suddenly had a scholarship to a local academy. The same academy his cousin went to.

To attend a school of this sort was one thing, dressing the part another. Handling the family's books, his Ma hocked one of their breeding sows against the debt, and got him clothes from the thrift-store. Two ill-fitting sports jackets, a couple of neckties, pants and a few dress shirts, but at least they weren't work clothes. Professional dry-cleaning beyond their means, she did her best to keep them clean and pressed.

Jake had to walk across the back fields early every morning, to catch the school's private bus on the lower road. His was the stop just beyond Mary Lu's. After a few questioning looks from the driver, Mary Lu's enthusiastic greeting seemed to answer some question the woman never vocalized. The next stop was almost five miles, down twisty country roads that bore little semblance of ever having been paved.

Old friends, it was perfectly natural for the youngsters to sit together and talk. Jake had always been fond of the girl, and now that she was in her teens there was so much more to be fond of. A true southern belle, she'd blossomed early. On nice spring days she'd get off at his stop, and they'd walk the half-mile to hers. It made him late for chores, but it was worth it. She was beautiful. He felt giddy just wandering along beside her. The boy was handsome too. Not that his African forebears had been ugly, but those roots had been diluted with the constant input of European linages, and the combination left him with a sort of virile yet attractive Mediterranean flavor.

They seldom discussed Mary Lu's home-life. She made it be known that it was bitter and then refused to talk about it. Her father was a domineering man, who'd beaten her mother into submission soon after their marriage. School had become the girl's escape, and now Jake her fascination. Bright, freckled, and sweet of nature, it was hard to imagine how she endured.

Mary Lu's laughter lifted Jake's spirit like birds of the field, and her smile filled him with a warmth he couldn't explain . . . until she kissed him. Barely a brush of his cheek in parting, yet to the boy the feeling was beyond anything he'd ever imagined.

Somehow his work got done that afternoon, but he had no memory of how. Preoccupied and silent through supper, Jake's mother felt his forehead a couple of times to make sure he hadn't taken a fever. Dead tired from another day in the fields, his father seldom had the energy to do much more than eat and sleep. He never noticed.

The boy helped clear the table, excused himself, then drifted toward his room, and the ever-waiting homework. Tonight's pages may as well have been written in Greek for all he got from them.

Sensing trouble, his mother slipped into the room and sat on the bed next to where he was working at his desk. She neither asked nor said a word, waiting until she was sure he was comfortable with her presence.

Instinctively aware that it was his move to make, he finally whispered, "She kissed me, Ma!"

His mother had no need to ask who. There were only three girls within walking distance, and two of them had yet to enter grade school. Heavy as stone, her heart felt like it was falling through the floor. She fought to hide the fear. "When?" was all she could muster.

"This afternoon. We walked from my bus-stop to hers, and when we stopped at the end of her driveway she kissed me goodbye!"

A measure of relief flooded the woman's body. She could breathe again. "It was just a kiss goodbye?"

"Yeah, but it ain't that simple!"

"What do you mean?" Tension returned to her voice.

"I love her, Ma! I've always loved her."

Head in hand, she said to him, "Jake, number one, she's your cousin, and besides, we've talked about your uncle before. He's got a temper worsen any man I know! He don't want nothin' to do with us 'ceptin' the money we bring him. The only reason he allows us to stay on his land is 'cause your grandfather made him promise. You start messin' 'round with Mary Lu, and he'll be rid of us quick."

"I'm sorry, Ma."

"We'll have to move! Your Daddy and me, we're doin' the best we can, but at our age I can't imagine startin' over someplace new. And, Missy Hills, what will she think after getting' you into that fancy school? Past your eighth grade, you've learned enough to work the fields with us, 'ceptin' I'd hoped so much more for you."

"I'm sorry, Ma. I'll tell her I can't see her no more!"

"If only life were that easy, Jake! Nature bein' what it is, I know it won't do no good to tell you to stay away from her, 'cause you cain't. The only thing I can ask is for you to think about what you're doin'. Not what your body's tellin' you, but what this means to all of us."

"Well, what am I gonna do?"

"Are you willing to live with what'll happen when you're found out? I'm tellin' ya, the girl's beyond you boy. You go there, and all it'll bring is a pile of hurt. You're the only rooster in the pen right now, but when she goes off to college she's gonna meet a lot of other boys. Young men with money, cars, and fancy clothes. She'll leave you feelin' like yesterday's newspaper in the bottom of a bird's cage. For the little bit of sweet-talk and humpin' a randy boy like you might get out of this, you're still gonna end up dirt-poor, and ridin' a plow in her daddy's fields."

"I know, Ma, but that don't keep her out of my head. I want to marry her!"

"Her daddy hears about this, you'll be lucky to have anything in that head! He wants to be our next State Rep. How far do you think he'd get if his fourteen year old daughter marries an octoroon first cousin?

*

Much as he tried to be indifferent, Mary Lu smiled at him when he joined her on the bus the next morning, and he was lost. He could feel his heart beating in his throat, and it took a conscious effort to breathe.

She babbled happily beside him, while he tried to think of a gentle way to tell her their friendship was over. The girl was looking at his face when she slipped her little finger around his, and held it tight. Hidden beneath the fluff of her skirt, none of the other kids could see.

His face burned. Without thinking, he took her hand and pressed it against his chino covered thigh. She smiled, and still hidden, rubbed her fingers against the warmth.

It was as if they'd never gone to school that day. Mary Lu was snuggled up against him when the bus driver pulled up to Jake's stop and opened the door. He smiled weakly at the operator, and thanked her as the two bounced down the steps together.

Now alone, the boy tried once more to explain why they shouldn't see each other again. Mary Lu heard him out, nodded as if she understood, and then wrapped her arms around him. They kissed. Kissed longingly, their bodies pressed against each other in the mindless passion of youth.

Coming up for air, he blurted, "We can't do this, Mary Lu!

Your father will kill us if he finds out!" He said one thing, but his arms still held her tightly.

She nibbled at his ear, "I know! And he really will, if he finds out. I've wanted to kiss you ever since I can remember. I love you Jake, and I don't care what Daddy says."

"But, Mary Lu!"

"Maybe we can run away, and get married!"

"I love you too, but we're only fourteen, Mary Lu! Ain't no preacher I know of will marry us without your Daddy's say so."

"We'll just run away then! We can get jobs in the city, and rent an apartment. Nobody's got to know we're not married!"

"Mary Lu, listen to yourself! It takes money to do that. I know my brother wanted to move to the city, but couldn't 'cause them landlords wanted the first and last month's rent, plus a security deposit. How we goin' to get that kinda money hawkin' po-boys? And what about you, goin' off to college? You can't give all that up! Look, I'll still be here when you graduate, and if you haven't found someone better by then, I'll be waiting."

A tear ran down her cheek as she announced, "Jake, I love you! I want you now, not eight years down the road! I want to live with you, have your babies, cook your dinner, and I sure don't want to go home again . . . ever."

He started to interrupt. "But. . . ."

"A lot can happen in eight years. We might be dead by then, without ever knowing what love is really like. I've never wanted anyone but you, and now . . . now you don't want me!" The tears began flowing like a spring rain. She muffled a sob as she pushed away from him.

He hurt inside. Good intentions washed away by her freshet, Jake drew her back into his arms.

Hearing a vehicle approach they ducked off the gravel pavement and hid behind the roadside brush.

*

The hayfield was still green this early in the season. She was warm and soft against him where they lay. The grass, a full two-and-a-half-feet high, hid them in a world of its own. Their ardor built to a frenzy, and she matched his heat with fire. Once enjoined, neither could let go 'til they had nothing left to give.

Afterwards, both lay naked, perspiring and exhausted in their sun-dappled nest. The smell of crushed grass hung sweetly in the air.

*

Jake never got to his chores that afternoon, and when he came to the supper table his mother only had to look at him to know. She didn't say a word, but he caught her dabbing at tears discreetly, so her husband wouldn't see. No need to worry father until the boss man was standing at their door. The meal passed quietly.

It rained the next day, but Mary Lu wasn't on the bus anyway. Coming over the last rise from the back fields, Jake felt relief when he saw his mother and father carrying groceries from their pickup into the house. By that simple act, it could be assumed they hadn't been evicted yet.

The rain meant the fields were too muddy to work. His father would have spent his day in the ramshackle barn out back, repairing machinery, or setting up a planter for the next crop to go in the ground. Caught up with those chores, he and Ma must have taken advantage of the weather and ridden into town. Trips like this gave Ma a chance to gossip and pick up needed supplies, while her husband could stop by the barbershop to discuss politics, prices, or the latest crop-pest.

As the boy stepped into the house, he sensed something wrong. Both parents wore grim faces, and there was little talk. It was only natural for Jake to think they'd discussed Mary Lu, and he girded for the worst.

"Hey, Ma! You been shoppin', huh?" Getting no response, the boy blurted out, "Is something wrong?"

His mother answered, "We just come by the tater field, and it looks like someone poked holes in the tractor's tires. Air was still bubblin' out of one of 'em. Don't know why anybody'd do somethin' like that. Tractor's our life's-blood!"

Jake's feelings were a mix of relief and distress.

DANCING NAKED

Edie May went on, "Tires that big take special machines to work on 'em. Stops rainin' by mornin', I'm goin' to have to help your father put the tractor on blocks, so we can pull the wheels and haul 'em to the repair shop. You'll have to get yourself off to school."

"I done that before, but why would somebody hurt the tractor? Was ours the only one got its tires flattened?"

"Don't know. Maybe the tire place can tell us."

*

Jake's mother came in the next morning to make sure he was awake before they left. The sound of their pickup hadn't much more than faded when he heard another truck's door slam. Curiosity dragged him from his bed to see where the noise had come from. Dressed only in boxer shorts, he wasn't much prepared for visitors.

Never locked, the door slammed open before he could reach it. A big hulk lumbered through the opening and blocked the light much as the closed door had before him. Jake froze for a second, then began to backpedal. From the look on his uncle's face, he had no need to ask what the man wanted.

Deceptively quick, his uncle reached out, grabbed Jake by the hair and slammed him against the wall. This was followed immediately with that bone crunching blow to his face. Dazed, blood spurted from his nose as the boy slid down the wall to the floor.

"Rape my daughter will you, you little nigger! You're going to have one sorry day in hell by the time I get through with you!"

The first kick caught him in the chest. The boy groaned at the sudden pain and struggled for air. The next one came quickly, and hurt even more. After a while they blended together, and Jake lost count. He lacked the breath to whimper at further insult so feigned death.

Not quite finished, the fellow stepped to the kitchen stove, opened the fire box and removed a scoop of glowing coals. A box of kindling and papers sat close at hand. It caught fast. Satisfied, the man walked out of the house, smug that there'd be no trace of accelerants and probably not even bones.

Jake had trouble breathing. His chest screamed. Daggers drove in to cut every attempt short. He forced an eye open. Everything was blurred. No air passed through his swollen nose, but something tasted bitter. Acrid actually, and then he began to hear the crackling noise. Sight obscuring smoke blinded his one good eye with tears.

Alarmed, he tried to lift his head to see, but the attempt produced agonizing pain and little movement.

He knew he had to get out. The boy grabbed at a table leg, and pulled himself toward the door. His body howled in protest. Smoke caught in his throat, but fear drove him forward as he clutched, grasped, and hauled at whatever was in reach. A smeared trail of blood marked his passage.

Closer now, the air was better. His uncle hadn't shut the inside door. A Godsend, because the boy could never have reached a doorknob.

Heat built from behind. He could hear things falling, and burning embers sprayed by in a mutual race for air, and life.

Jake began fading in and out. Everything hurt so. He could see through the screen door to the worn steps leading down off their porch.

Close! So close. . . .

*

The tire repairs had cost them fifty dollars. Money, hard to come by, and irreplaceable. Of more concern was that no other tractors had been vandalized that day, but the repairman said it was still early. Then he showed them the thirty-two caliber slugs he'd found in each tire, and suggested they call the police.

Short of bringing his workhorse home each night, there was little Jake's dad could do to prevent a reoccurrence.

Their truck rattled up the dirt road, and suddenly the young man's mother began to scream. The white smoke lingered like a bank of fog as it wafted lazily through the long-leaf pines. A half-mile from the house, she had no doubt as to where it had come from.

*

Mary Lu came home late from school that day. Very late.

She didn't know the bus driver had met her father at the Quick Store earlier. The woman had sought him out and asked, "That there Mary Lu's cousin I pick up down the road, he a bit dusky, ain't he?"

Not happy about being reminded of something he'd hoped everyone else had forgotten, his answer was surly. "Yeah, what about it?"

"Ah knew it. Ah knew I shouldn't a let him on my bus. How'd he get inta dat school? I gotta talk ta some people. Actin' the white boy, he ain't gonna get me in no trouble for it. Oh, an by da way, I tink dat niggah putting the sweet talk on your lil' girl. Gettin' uppity, somebody otta put the fear of God back in him so he remember his place in dis world."

The enraged man flew home to confront his offspring, and got there first. She appeared disheveled when he opened the door to let her in. He asked bluntly where she'd been. Caught and in a panic, Mary Lu mumbled something about the bus had broken down.

Her father's shouts of anger were so vehement as to be unintelligible. He demanded the girl have an immediate exam by their family doctor.

Hysterical, the girl was given a sedative to calm her long enough for the procedure.

The doctor confirmed the obvious. Thinking quickly, her father alluded to the boy responsible as being one of Mary Lu's classmates, and said his father was a man who wielded great political power. He also claimed to have already spoken with this fellow, and the two of them decided that Mary Lu should be institutionalized in a hospital where the man had influence. That way her emotional state could recover, and the hospital would take care of any unfortunate miscarriages.

The family doctor raised an eyebrow at what was being suggested, but said nothing.

Lies were a regular part of her father's world. He never noticed the reaction. Besides, he had already formulated a more practical solution to his problem. Hospitals cost money. If Mary Lu was pregnant, her illegitimate child wouldn't be the first to be born at home.

With no guarantee either way, the man knew for sure who the father was not going to be. It mattered little that the girl claimed to love Jake, theirs was not an arrangement he could ever acknowledge.

On the way home, the man bought a new box of high-powered, .32 cal. cartridges for the ever-present rifle hanging across his truck's rear window. Enough power to drop a coyote or deer in its tracks, he figured they'd penetrate a tractor's tire just as easily . . . or maybe a boy, if given the chance.

If that should happen he'd claim rape, and who would blame him. In fact, that might buy some sympathy votes. Mary Lu could have her child, and he'd be given credit for doing what was right by bringing up their bastard as his own.

In his mind, things were getting better all the time.

*

Jake's mother flew out of the pickup and ran toward the pile of smoldering timbers and ash that once had been a home. The woman screamed for her son, hoping against hope that he'd left for school before calamity struck.

Her husband followed. He kicked at the rubble, head down, shoulders slumped, a beaten man. Two children dead, maybe three, and their houseful of memories turned to smoke.

The sound was a strangled scream. Different enough to have the man's head whip towards his wife. She sat there, back to him, cradling something in her lap.

He couldn't believe the ash-covered body still had life in it. As the man dropped to his knees, tears washed a minuscule amount of the foulness from his remaining child's face. Jake was trying to apologize, saying he was sorry to have brung this wrath upon the family. Then he went on to name the man who had tried to kill him.

The voice wasn't strong enough for his father to hear, but the look on Ma's face said she hadn't missed a word. The old man's thoughts were on the nearest hospital. Questions could wait. With Ma's help, he got his son over his back, staggered the fifty yards or so to the truck, and eased the boy onto its rusted bed. Jake's mother climbed in beside her boy to cushion his head.

*

She knew what had to be done. It was her kin, her responsibility. While her husband went through the ruins with the authorities, she walked out to the back fields to get away from everything for a little while.

A half-mile up from Jake's bus-stop was the drive. His mother was sweating from the heat and effort of her walk. The back of her housedress was wet through, and a drip of perspiration hung from a curly-cued wisp of hair that dangled down her forehead.

Her half-brother's shiny new pickup sat there in the shade, its windows open.

Answering the knock on his door personally, the man never had a chance. He made a desperate grab for the gun. The explosion was loud. She flinched, but never moved. The slug from his own rifle caught him just under the chin and drove upward.

Unguided, his dead hand completed its last task by yanking the weapon from Edie May's grasp. Falling away from her, he twisted, the rifle landing beneath his body on the floor.

*

An immediate, on-site inquiry assumed the man had heard about his imminent arrest. Suicide was listed as the official cause of death. The follow-up investigation provided one other interesting twist. An old will was found mixed in with insurance policies and the like. It seems that upon his death, Jake's grandfather had always intended for his estate to be divided equally, between both of his children.

Mary Lu's father, named executor, had never bothered to file the legal document.

DANCING NAKED

THE SECRET

Today is Saturday.

I'm sitting on a curb surrounding a rotary in the town of Felipe Carrillo Puerto in southern Quintanna Roo, Mexico. I've been here before . . . the first time was almost a half a century ago— searching for the devil that had lingered in my mind, taxing my sanity since my youth.

This town is very old, populated primarily by hard-working Mayans who worship a talking cross housed in an old stucco church across the rotary and down the street from where I sit; the **Iglesia de la Cruz** *with wide-eyed, deep set windows.*

This is real Mexico, untouched by tourist development; no beach or ancient ruins to lure the tourists, so it is likely to stay this way. It could be a site of interest for travelers, if interested travelers ever came here. When I first visited in 1967 there was an old priest who served the masses from this church. His name was Father Prudencio Melguíades. He had been here for fifty-six years— since 1911.

Directly in the middle of the rotary is a ten-foot tall bronze statue of Presidente Benito Juárez. He was a Zapotec Indian who ruled Mexico during the mid to late 1800s, a major political feat in those days; impossible today. I have learned much about the Indians of Mexico . . . the Maya, the Aztecs and the Zapotecs. Many Indians from this town migrated north to Mexico City to find wealth and safety. Most returned because it wasn't there, not for them. Felipe Carrillo Puerto has not changed since Juárez.

There is little to see here, after you see the Juarez statute.   But I am very happy; content. And so I sit here. My huaraches are in the car because I like the feel of my bare feet touching the ground, like long ago dancing naked with a woman.

Benito is watching me.   He knows my secret.

DANCING NAKED

***

I speak Spanish fluently because when I was seventeen years old I lived in Mexico for thirteen months as an exchange student. Early on during that year, I impregnated a woman three years my senior. It was my introduction to sex. Not her's, of that I am now certain. When she told me she was pregnant, my first instinct was to run and hide. *Embarazada.* But I came from the Presbyterian Midwest and Boy Scout Troop #79. In those days, boys—young men—from my town were taught to live with their mistakes. It was an issue of honor. I wasn't sure what I should do. I thought perhaps it would work itself out . . . somehow. The Cisco Kid promised all good cowboys that good would come to them, so I believed that everything would be all right.

***

Her name was Carmencita Trejo of Indian heritage . . . Zapotecan, she said; carefree, childlike, painted lips, perfect teeth and soft, black, corn-silk hair she would toss from her face with a quick shake of her head. I moved in with her yet still attended classes as if nothing had happened. Never told anyone at school about it; never wrote home about it. I waited for IT to fix itself. IT—the mess. She went to work each day. We lived in a small one-room apartment in the basement of a tenement house near her family. For seven months we were speechless Ozzie and Harriets in heat . . . anxious, dry-mouthed, wet-bodied. Humping like wild animals, knocking over lamps and breaking our one kitchen chair. Then sleeping.

    On May 10, 1957 we had a very pre-mature boy. I held him that day, and his heart became embedded in mine; tentacled, so to speak. His eyes touched my eyes, forming a lasting memory. Curious black pupils seeking, communicating; so strange. I would never forget that moment.

DANCING NAKED

July 28, 1957, 4:12 A.M. I awoke, startled. Something moved our bed. The ground, buildings, everything began to shudder, tremble, then jolt and shake. Walls collapsed and floors turned to dust. I scampered to the floor, groggy from sleep just as our ceiling fell like a massive guillotine. Carmencita died beneath the rubble of our basement apartment, a large ceiling beam crushed her face beyond recognition.

The child had fallen to the floor unharmed, screaming. I was too stunned to react, numbed by the sight of death. Stone silence followed . . . an inside-the-casket hush. And then the roar . . . Oh, God, the roar! Voices from the street yelled, *"El fin del mundo"* (the end of the world). It happened all too fast. A rampaging eddy of sounds and thoughts, and me carrying a two-month-old child wrapped in a bloody blanket, wandering the early morning streets rampant with tipped automobiles, smoke, debris and the smells ... musk, burned fat, carrion, singed hair, charred electricity. *Un terremoto*, they said. I didn't know what it meant. I needed help. Where would I go? Sirens screamed in the streets, people moaned and cried and fell to their knees in prayer, hands to the sky. "Where are you, God?" one woman shouted. This was bigger than anything human—louder, more rancid, evil.

I took the child to Carmencita's parents' apartment. It was a dingy, tin-roofed small shack like most dwellings of the native Indians in that country. Somehow they had survived. More confusion, hysterics, and panic followed. *Carmencita se me ha muerto* (Carmencita is dead), I told them. Their daughter—dead. Dead! DEAD! They cried, fell to the floor, holding each other, mourning, lamenting. Then "fault" arose. Whose fault? The boy's. The gringo. Their eyes glared as if I had done it. Whispering to each other, they snatched the infant from my arms and told me to go away. *"Que vayas tu. Niño!"* (Go away little boy), they said, disgusted with my naiveté and immaturity. They would raise the child.

DANCING NAKED

Frantically they took everything I had as if in repayment for their daughter . . . my wallet, passport, belt (with sterling silver buckle), and all the money my family had given me.

I wandered down *Avenida Insurgentes* alone but strangely relieved because I had found a home for the child—my child. He would be better off with his "own kind" my self-talk uttered, desperately looking for a way out. After all, I was seventeen and in the early stages of a long-term nightmare.

For a time, which I cannot define, my mind was an empty envelope. I wandered and became sick from shared alcohol, bad food and curb-side water. Screaming pain began to grip my penis when I urinated ... harsh like a wire brush roto-rooter in my urethra. Eventually I found myself barely standing in Alameda Park, downtown Mexico City unable to stop my diarrhea and awaken from this nightmare. All that was left were voices that talked to me from mouths that never moved and abstract images of naked, headless Mayans running in darkness to nowhere. Someone stopped me from dancing naked in the park, the way I danced with Carmencita and took me to the American Red Cross, which had been searching for me for a month. Without a passport, they were unable to identify me. Then to a hospital with broken windows and white curtains that luffed. Footsteps echoed down granite hallways like fingernails tapping desktops. And the sounds and smells of forced cleanliness. The diagnosis hanging at the foot of my bed listed three diseases: amoebic dysentery, gonorrhea, and malnutrition. The first two I had never heard of.

***

I was returned to the states through the American Embassy, my identity affirmed. Daniel Wallace. My family was relieved and concerned. I had survived *El Terremoto* of 1957. The Guerrero Earthquake. I would wear it like a merit badge.

Mom and Dad were proud of me and told their friends that it would be some time before I got over this "horrible nightmare." How blessed we were that I had no serious physical injuries, only severe amoebic dysentery which could be treated. The recurring memory, though, of giving away my child could never be treated. I could never tell anyone. I would put that part of the story away forever.

My doctor gave me 3 vials of pills, 2 for the dysentery and 1 for the gonorrhea. "I don't know how long you've had gonorrhea," the doctor said. "Do you?"

"What is it?" I asked.

I watched a giant eye-roll unfurl. "Gonorrhea is a sexually transmitted disease, young man. You probably know it as the Clap. You've got one of the worst cases I've ever seen, obviously unchecked for sometime."

I stared straight ahead—paralyzed, knowing I did not want to do eye contact with this man.

"You didn't know?" he asked.

"No, sir. Not really."

"Gonorrhea is a contagious disease one gets from sexual intercourse with an unclean partner."

My brain jolted and echoed: *An unclean partner.*

"Mom and Dad know?" I asked.

"Of course they know."

The doctor told my Mom and Dad that I was seriously depressed. ". . . and for good reason," he added. "That was a traumatic event for a seventeen year old." The next day my medication was increased to include an anti-depressant.

***

I never told anyone about the woman or the child because I wasn't certain they ever existed. Their images arrived vividly in the night, subtly. Yet when I stood in front of a mirror—in the quiet, my mind slowing, — I knew it was real. My eyes told me. Scenes of naked barefoot dancing, then of panic and voices raced through my head . . . of handing my child to someone else. Giving away my purpose. And painful days of urinating while driving my fingers into my ears to divert the pain.

   Gonorrhea.

An unclean woman.

Was I the goat, the fool?

   Yet a drop of my blood still lived in Mexico, a drop I couldn't wash away. I wasn't sure the child had a name. Carmencita called him Chato because of his flat nose. When I held him, I was his proud father. His padre. I became a silent zombie, afraid of the memory. The fear of a nightmare created insomnia. The *dancer in the dark* and our child became unerasable tattoos etched into my heart.

   "What can your mother and I do for you, Dan?" my father asked, reaching out awkwardly. He would never be able to handle the truth.

   "I'm fine," I replied . . . replied because I was certain no one would understand . . . if they were ever to believe me. *You had an illegitimate child from an unclean woman that you were living with, and you gave the child away? You don't know where your child is? You must be a cold-hearted moron.*

   "I don't mean to argue with you, but you're not okay." Dad's eyes sagged at the far corners squinching his forehead. Sympathy. How deeply he wanted to fix things. That's what fathers are supposed to do. I couldn't fix my son's troubles either, so I gave them away in that rundown hovel to two *Indios,* parents of this girl who infected me.

   That was when I locked the door and vowed not to peep into that room again. The room of betrayal and shame. All that was left of Mexico was the language. That would not go away.

Whenever I heard people speak it, I was drawn to them like a magnet. I couldn't wait to speak that language. It was like scratching poison ivy; thinking of it made it worse. But the child . . . rocking in his cradle of hypocrisy. Chato—flat nose.

I left him as casually as one leaves a tip for a ham sandwich.

***

My senior year in college I took a course on the history of Mexico, from the Aztecs to Miguel Alemán. There was a full chapter on the Zapotec Indians and their hero, Benito Juárez, president of Mexico. I devoured that chapter and haunted the library looking at pictures of Zapotec Indians. I mentally changed their hair styles and put different clothes on them, like a child with paper dolls, comparing them to Carmencita and her family.

I dropped the course after I first drew pictures—one a light brown woman with glossy black pubic hair—that looked like they came from some mental ward.

***

After college I took a job in New York City. Mom and Dad visited me once a year. We went out to nice restaurants, had too much to drink and then to the theater. The past; Mexico, the earthquake and gonorrhea were never discussed. But I could see the question marks in their eyes. My past was past.

In 1967 Dad called, saying he was going to be in the city on business and would I have dinner with him.

The tablecloths at the Gramercy Park Hotel restaurant were linen and pressed and the water glasses filled, moist and cold. Dad slid an envelope addressed to me—Sr. Daniel William Wallace—across the table. It had been previously opened. I turned it over and read the return address. *Instituto Nacional de Migración* (Mexican Department of Immigration). Fear began its descent. A crumpled letter was stuffed inside addressed to me with the heading, *Prensa de Ley de Nacionalidad de Mexico* (News of the

Nationality law). The letter stated that new changes in the immigration laws required this correspondence to non-citizens of Mexico. That since I was married to a deceased Mexican person and had sired a Mexican child, I could maintain dual citizenship. The letter listed Carmencita Trejo as my deceased wife and a son listed as Ernesto Wallace y Trejo. Oh my God, It was Chato! A deep breath caught half way and I stopped breathing. A memory forged of a Priest in the hospital writing the baby's name on an official document. Ernesto Wallace y Trejo. A dread roiled.

    The document explained that Chato was living with a grandmother, Anna Trejo de Itzamna in the town of Felipe Carrillo Puerto. Paralyzed I could only stare at the paper and my trembling hands, holding it. My mind raced, caved in, ached. It had been ten years, and I thought I had begun to put that event into perspective. Tucked it away as of no consequence. Just a tough break. There was nothing I could do about it. It was over. Carmencita was who she was. It no longer mattered. I did have a child but chances of locating him were remote. But then, still from time to time, painful voices from the past dragged images across my mind. Headless sights and sounds driven by remorse, regret and doubt.

    I looked up, expressionless, from the letter at Dad and a feeling of panic set in. Something was taking over. I grabbed my mouth and squeezed . . . squeezed my fingers deep into my cheeks until they wanted to bleed, wanting pain to erase everything. My head trembled and my eyes shook in their sockets, expanding, ready to pop from their nests. Tears came from my heart in droves and covered my vision, running down my cheeks, over my hand to the linen tablecloth.

    Life had caught up with me. My heart was exposed.

    "You all right?" Dad asked.

I shook my head *No*, staring out at images from inside a fish bowl.

"I didn't mean for this to happen . . . like this," he said. "I thought we would talk about it."

All I could do was nod. Words were still eddies of dried saliva.

We walked through Gramercy Park as the sun went down and the street lights came on. Pastel hues fell from the park lamps like talcum powder falling from a woman's face.

"It's true," I said faintly—finally.

"God," Dad breathed. "And you've been carrying this ever since then?"

I nodded. An old man shuffled by barefoot.

"Anyone else know about this?"

"Not a soul."

We walked in silence.

"Oh, son. What a burden for you." He put his arm around my shoulder and pulled me close to him. It felt reassuring . . . a first for us. I turned and hugged him. Never before had we been affectionate. I rested my weight on his shoulders, relaxed and sobbed. He patted and rubbed my back, awkwardly at first, then like a pro. A first for him. "What a burden," he whispered. "What a fucking burden."

"It's been difficult." Me. Whispering, sniffing still.

"Who was the woman?"

I pointed to a park bench. We sat and I told him everything. The first time I met her, Hotel de Cortez, Zapotec Indians of Mexico, sex, dancing naked in her apartment, her pregnancy, the baby, Chato, the earthquake, her smashed face peering lifeless, bloody blankets, her devastated parents. I talked about my guilt, my shame, my unwillingness to say anything to anyone.

"I read somewhere that there is a mystical adhesion that happens when a parent first holds its child," Dad said. "I could never put you out of my mind, son . . . never forget that moment in the hospital when I first held you. My son . . ." he nodded, his chin wrinkling in emotion. ". . . I could never walk away from you, just as you could never walk away from your son. Just as God can not walk away from His children."

That night Dad stayed at my apartment. We drank sour mash whiskey and talked about "remember when." And suddenly like the snow settling inside a glass paper weight clearly revealing a lone figure. That figure was my father . . . representing all those things I never imagined or allowed him to represent.

"Son, I don't mean to tell you what to do, but you need to get on an airplane and fly to this little shit-assed town. Wherever the hell it is."

FELIPE CARILLO PUERTO, 1967

From the airport in Cancun, I drove south away from the commercial glitz. Three hours of rainless, windless white-knuckle driving . . . driving in my own fear-storm. Gradually the road became less populated and more densely foliaged; past the ruins of the Maya village of Tulum where the road begins to be squeezed by the jungle. Little black butterflies sun themselves on the pavement in June and try to avoid speeding cars. Many meet their fate on the windshield becoming opaque smears, causing me to turn on my wipers and further obscure the view. The foliage is heavy here, summery rich . . . deep, old green. Then the road runs flat like a sleeping snake to Felipe Carrillo Puerto.

I had no idea what I would do when I arrived in the town. Should I tell him I was his father? Should I speak to his grandparents? Should I give them some money? How would I locate them? Is there a phone book in Felipe Carrillo Puerto? Do the—what's their names?—the Trejos—have a telephone? Do they still live there? Three hours I planned and plotted, took notes, scratched out bad ideas until there were no ideas left. And then there I was at the rotary facing Presidente Benito Juaréz. For the first time in ten years I took off my shoes and socks and smiled.

    A dog-eared phone book listed eight Trejos, not one Anna and I didn't know the grandfather's name. Several Itzamnas but nothing like Anna Trejo de Itzamna. Ten thousand people, mostly of Mayan descent, lived in this town. I watched everyone looking for a clue and drank heavily that afternoon. I asked the waitress if she was familiar with a Trejo family living in town. She smiled politely, knew a young couple in Isla Mujeres named Trejo, but had never heard of any in this town. I checked into the best of two hotels downtown. At the desk I asked if the desk clerk knew Anna Trejo de Itzamna. Blank looks and shaking heads. The same reaction at breakfast from the waitress. When I paid my bill she suggested I go to the Church of the Cross (*Iglesia de la Cruz*) and talk to Father Prudencio because he had lived in Felipe Carillo Puerto for many years.

    I walked down the street, around the rotary and up a side street to the Iglesia de la Cruz, a small adobe-styled white stucco church with a bruised wooden door that pushed open begrudgingly, and its sound echoed throughout the stark interior where harsh sounding floors and butt-polished pews of ebony lent a sacred aura. A carved confessional sat at the far end of the nave emitting low mumblings. You could almost hear the beads rattling. I stayed in the back of the church waiting. Soon the confessional door opened and a small man in light brown priests' robes shuffled out, head bowed, hands folded in front.

    I approached him along a narrow aisle to the side. At first he was suspicious, and for good reason, I was a blonde-haired blue-eyed American in sneakers. But my accent was very Mexican . . . low class Mexican. I was one of the guys . . . just painted differently. He motioned us outside to a garden walkway.

"Who is this child you look for?" he asked, squinting in the bright sunlight.

"He is my son, Chato. I have not seen him since he was two months old in Mexico City. The immigration people say he and his grandparents live in this town."

"He would be how old?"

"He was ten years old May 10th."

"And his mama?"

"She died in the terremoto of 1957."

"I am so sorry." He said guiding along a garden pathway.

"Me, too," I mumbled, not sure if I really was.

"After all these years, why do you now look for this boy? This is like (then in English; very rough English)—as you say in America—looking for a needle in a haystick."

"That's haystack," I corrected, grinning. "*Almiar*."

"*Almiar*. Haystack. *Es verdad?* Is that true?" His face lit up and he giggled, secular-like.

"That's right," I said. "There are no needles in hay*sticks*."

" Only haystacks."

"*Sí*."

Then in Spanish, he continued. "This might be just as difficult. Why do you look for him?"

"That's a long story, Father. He has been in my heart, talking to me since I left him with his grandparents 10 years ago."

"And if you find this child, what will you tell him."

I looked around the garden. "I'm not sure. Maybe nothing. I just need to see him. To know that he's all right. I think it will help me get my life back in order."

"You are not doing it for the child, you are doing it for yourself, right?"

"You're probably right. Is that selfish?"

"No. I would not say so," He said.

"His grandmother is Anna Trejo y Itzamna." I said.

"Her mother was Mayan." Father said.

"Is that a question? Or did you know her?"

"Itzamna is a Mayan name."

"I thought she was Zapotec." I said.

"Who?"

"Carmencita. She was the boy's mother."

"You were married?" He asked.

"No, Father. I got her pregnant and we lived together."

"This is very bad, you know." He said, shaking his head slowly and sucking his teeth.

"Yes, I know. Father, I hardly knew her. I'm not sure she loved me, and I was only seventeen. You don't think right at that age around a beautiful woman. But I have been haunted by it, day and night."

"Do you think right around beautiful women now?" He grinned.

"Probably not. Maybe a little better."

"Come with me," he said, putting his hand on my back and turning to the church, stiffening my anti-spiritual resolve.

"Father, I'm not much of a believer. I really don't want to go into church, kneel and pray."

"Oh I know that. It's too bright out here and I can't see your eyes to know if you are speaking the truth."

"I am speaking truthfully. I swear to you I am. I am frustrated and confused. I thought this would be easy."

We walked back into the church in silence, his hand quietly on my back, patting. I wondered if he knew or if he did know, would he tell me. The church was empty. The candles glowed and he turned on the lights, brightening the sanctuary.

"There. Much better." Then he mumbled something I couldn't hear.

"What?" I asked.

"*Los dos sabía que.* I knew them both," he said quietly, turning to face me, his hands on my arms.

"*Los dos?*"

"Yes. Anna and young Ernesto—your son. I was here long before they returned from the city. This is where Anna's family lived. I knew Marcos from many years before."

"Marcos?"

"Anna's husband. *He* was Zapotec. He died in the city soon after the terremoto of 1957 and Anna returned to her home with the grandchild."

"How long ago was that, Father?"

"Little Ernesto was maybe two."

"Carmencita and I called him Chato. I had blocked out his real name. I was trying to block out everything."

"Anna never told anyone about the child," he continued. "Only that their daughter and her husband—you—were killed in the terremoto."

"She kept it inside." I understood too well.

"An unspoken lie is a terrible burden. She carried her's until she became ill. That's when she confessed her sin of lying to me," he said.

"Oh, God. I hurt so much, Father. What should I do?"

"Anna prayed for Ernesto, that he would be legitimized. I can't do that. What is done is done. It is in God's hands. She mailed your passport to the *Instituto Nacional de Migración* with a letter that said you were the husband and father."

"Where is Anna now?"

"She is buried in a small family graveyard in Ocum about 3 kilometers south."

"What about my son?"

"Your son is fine. He lives with an aunt in Ocum. He is such a charming young man. He is often doing jobs in this town or washing car windows near the town square. He does well for his family, being just ten years old. Come, I have to sit down now. Do not worry. We will not pray. I will wait until you leave."

I chuckled. "*Gracias, padre.*"

We walked down the center aisle of the church and he sat in the front pew.

"Do you know the nickname for Ernesto?" he asked, motioning for me to sit next to him.

"I don't think so."

"Che," He said.

"Che? As in Che Guevara?"

"That's correct. Such an honor in our culture to carry that great revolutionary's name. You will hear your son referred to as Che. You should be very proud of your son."

I sat next to Father Prudencio in silence, listening to the faulty electricity sputter and mice running somewhere near by. Mostly I listened to my heart beat—thumping like a finale. I liked being proud of my son.

"What will you do?" he asked.

Words were not there, only my slowly moving head from side to side. "What's he know about his father?" I finally asked.

"Only that he was great man, killed in the *terremoto* of 1957 and that his father—you—named his son after that great revolutionary leader at Castro's side. Your image is that of a great American expatriate, fighting for the rights of the poor."

An elderly woman in dark rags and torn sweater shuffled down the aisle, barefoot. Father Prudencio stood up. He put his hand on my shoulder. "We will stay in touch. For now, go with God, my son."

"Thank you."

***

I took a bottle of beer from a bar in town and sat on a bench in the *zocalo*. Small Christmas tree lights were draped through the trees and tired leaves fell from a fig tree like downed helicopters. Music wafted from afar and the lingering smell of sewage faintly passed through. *A great American expatriate, fighting for the rights of the poor.* There are many ways to translate a story from one language to the next, but translating "advertising copywriter who ditched his son" to "great American hero" was not going to work.

I would not burst that kid's bubble and tell him his father was simply a less-than-average guy. But I couldn't leave Felipe Carillo Puerto until I saw him.

The next day at lunch Father Prudencio stopped by my table and sat. He looked at me and grinned, and he shook his head. "I never ever imagined God would have blessed me with these few days . . . that I would meet young Che's father and know that he will be fine from now on . . . Che and his papa."

"From now on is a long time Father," I said.

He patted my hands. "Che is playing baseball in the field across from the church. You will recognize him because of your heart."

I didn't even thank the Father. I got up quickly and jogged up the street to the church. Ten children were playing baseball. They were all of Indian descent . . . dark skin, soft black hair, high cheek bones, crooked teeth and flat noses. What happened to my genes? I wondered. No baseball gloves, an old worn baseball and a fine Louisville Slugger.

DANCING NAKED

Soon someone hit a long drive near me and one of the children raced after it. He paused momentarily picked it up and looked at me.

The invisible thread grew taut. Dad was right.

Here was Ernesto "Che" Wallace y Trejo de Itzamna. It was as if I was looking through a mirror at the inside of the backside of my life, at a child I supposedly had sired, not fathered, yet loved none-the-less . . . more than I loved anyone, at that point.

"Che!" One of the other children yelled. "Throw it here."

END

DANCING NAKED

THE GIFT

My sightless dog, Ticket, falters over the rotted ties. I don't remember this path into the woods along the railroad bed being so long. On a leash, I help to guide her where we once walked many years ago, unleashed, scampering, eager. Should I carry her toward the grassy path or leave her to enjoy the earthy smells on her own? There were never the beer cans or bits of flotsam as there are now. That was so long ago. We venture out later in the day because the darkness before dawn may be a challenge to both of us now. Will that mean I will miss the activity? I hope not. Now we walk slowly, stepping more cautiously toward the red maple swamp.

Twenty years ago, my dog, Puki, ran freely, and then waggingly, happily returned to my side. She wiggled past the bushes into the muddy swamp, enjoying the cool muck of the warm pre-dawn day. Damp Spring smells aroused her curiosity. Me, too. Before the leaves had come out, the dog and I had the earth to ourselves with other plans, for this was a prime birding spot for early spring warblers to rest and revive on their way to Canada or other points north.

    Then, my purpose also was to find solitude to shed the tears of desperation that welled up in the black depression that was haunting me for too long. Daily, I hid these emotions as much as I could, but there were times when there was no stopping. Seemed that they determined my life, rather than the other way around. This path was soaked so often with the wails of my pain. In this seclusion, I could very well allow familiar sounds to me, but to nobody else. Escape. Safe.

   Bird life. They congregate in a secretive mass of glory.
   Potato chip . . . dip, potato chip . . . dip, potato chip . . . dip. That is the flight pattern of the eastern goldfinch. Just watch it. You will see. A chickadee tumbles from one branch to another almost without the most minute spread of wings. A great blue heron leans forward on its lanky legs and extends its long graceful wings to lift itself into the air. A downy or larger hairy woodpecker tucks its wings tightly against its body to dart toward the proposed tree. Just as it comes close enough, it opens its wings to put on the brakes and lands at its goal. Each has a different pattern. Early morning offers the most ambitious sightings. A nuthatch peeks upward from its down-turned body while it clutches the upright wood. A red-tailed hawk soars 'round about the new daylight in a cloudless spiral and suddenly dives toward its prey. All day the business of birds occurs. No sense of economy, flustering, blustering.

May ninth is generally a feathery, colorful tiny debut, so yearly I reserve the day to view the party, to pull me away from myself. Here in the depths of this tiny neighborhood, rich with safety, the racket is luscious and alluring with birdsong. Wiping away the tears, gathering up my gasps, I raised binoculars to the familiar song of the black and white warbler, the tiniest of birds. Sure enough. He flits along the lower branches of a nearby bush. I can separate the day's internal pain by enjoying the glory of what nature offers. And a yellow! A blackburnian!

The railroad bed was long enough for release of the main purpose of my being there. No counseling helped me through this dark period in my life. There was no direction but into the depth of the dark morning woods for the bird sightings that gave me the lift to what was the best of life. A respite from frailty. If they could flit in glorious parade in front of my eyes, how could I wallow in sorrow for myself?

And an American redstart!

I hear a vireo, dig out my book, (a Peterson's Guide) to decide which one.

Could I match the sound and the markings for another first for my life list? I surely hope so. This curiosity for gentle joys wrenched me toward a healing. A tiny healing daily, but a healing, nonetheless. I grab hold of the glorious hymn of birdsong entering my body for some sort of balance, pleased to think that I have just begun to stand on my feet, head above, a semblance of wholeness.

I have a life list that offers me remembrances of places I have traveled to see these beauties. Where someone else may have small shots of bird visions, mine are the formation of my health. They are the symbols of freedom from, well, freedom.

A personal life list is a written record that tells the first identification of that species, where I spied a particular bird, when by date and what it was doing at the time. It may not tell whether male or female, but that I saw it. That was all I needed. I needn't remind myself of what I was doing, because I know each and every time I was saving myself. I grabbed onto the miracle of nature that brought color and brilliance to my world. I was saving myself. They were offering me a simple leg-hold on the upward journey of mind above body.

DANCING NAKED

A doggy ruckus has erupted ahead! . . . and I pushed aside my book to see. I walk quietly toward the event. Puki has rustled up a young family of woodcocks, the mother portraying a wounded soul, her broken wing dance luring us away from her brood. I know the ruse. She flutters distraughtly in a dance of near death, round and round on the ground, spinning away from the little brown fluffs of down, hoping that they will be saved, hoping that the enemy will not wander from her drama. She is the star of this histrionic show. I look on, holding fast to my old dog. Sure enough, in the dark, crisp leaves nearby, I spy maybe seven or eight . . . nine tiny chicks.

Motherhood is ultimately the force that makes most of us survive. I am bereft of my own motherhood. I am the wounded winged mother who has lost her own family. But I had been a ferocious advocate for her short life. Surviving this struggle may have seemed fruitless at times, but my broken winged fight lives on. I can be a woodcock, a model of self protection.

She is something to watch in silence from my height until she lies silently on her side, resting and determining the quiet instant when she may return to her family. They scurry away together into the safety of the woods as I head back to the maple swamp.

A scarlet tanager slips through a lone white birch above. The contrast is startling. I am alive and aware. The dog has shown me her prize and then runs off to roll in some dead and very smelly animal carcass. Oh, the joys of being a dog!

So much for the vireo. My car will be rank on the way home unless I can entice her into the pond nearby, cold 'though it may be. All will soon be quiet.

DANCING NAKED

Sometimes I think they know, for how else would I be so fortunate to see so much when others do not.

    Their stage is my vision. My vision is their stage.

And that is what I remember now, reminding me that this late morning walk with Ticket will not provide an ornithological journey, but a fond remembrance of one long last day when the earth and its inhabitants saved my life. My mood is on better things now. I have emotional stability most of the time. Nothing is as difficult. We turn and slowly make our way back to the car.

DANCING NAKED

DANCING NAKED

SALVATION SOLL

Each Christmas Eve, when the boys sat cross-legged on the floor, eyes wide, their father told the story a bit differently – except for the ending. Adam added humor or invented dialogue here and there. He omitted dicey details. But he never wavered when he explained how he met Samaria, Jake and Joshua's mother. That part was sacred.

Before Adam first told his sons the story of Salvation Soll, they sat down to the traditional Italian Christmas Eve meal Adam grew up with, the Feast of the Seven Fishes – *Festa dei sette pesci*. It commemorates the wait -- *Vigilia di Natale* -- for the midnight birth of the baby Jesus. This Christmas Eve menu only lasted two years in the Delmonico household.

"Tell them, Jake," Joshua said that second year, as he looked at the calamari and shrimp in his plate. Joshua, 8, was the pensive, quiet son who spent hours reading *The Extraordinary Adventures of Ordinary Boy*.

"No, you tell them," Jake said.

"No. It was your idea."

"Tell us what?" Adam said as he forked a piece of fried cod.

"Well, Dad," Jake began. "I mean, please don't be offended. I know you told us last year how much the Seven Fishes means to you. But…"

Jake, 6, was the extrovert whose intelligence left many an adult with mouth agape. He considered *Captain Underpants* "too juvenile" and would rather read *The Hobbit.* Jerry the next-door neighbor hollared, "Hey Jakepedia, whattayaknow," whenever he saw Jake, who under his breath, answered, "I know you annoy me" or "I know where I'd like to send you." Sam called her son, "Our little genius."

"More like our pain in the butt," his brother said.

"No worries, buddy," Adam said. "Go ahead. Tell us what's on your mind."

"We really don't like the Seven Fishes deal, Dad," Jake said.

"Yeah," chimed in Joshua. "Don't really like it."

"We'd much rather have a Feast of the Eight Slices," Jake said.

Sam tried to stifle her laugh, and nearly spit out a piece of salted cod.

Adam glared at her, then at his sons.

"I mean, did your dad make you eat squid when you were a little kid?" Jake said.

"Sure did. And if I didn't eat it, my father would--- No, I didn't like it, either. Point taken."

Adam laughed. "If that's what you guys want," he said. "Done. Starting next Christmas, pizza."

Joshua and Jake then ate everything on their plates, even the fried squid.

"Story time?" Jake said when dinner was finished.

"Story time," his father said.

"And then dessert," Sam said as she picked up the boys' dishes. "Fish cakes."

"Nice try, mom," Jake said.

The boys sat beside the Christmas tree while Adam placed dishes in the dishwasher and Sam spooned leftover fish, shrimp and calamari into containers and put them in the refrigerator.

Adam grabbed a bottle of beer, Sam poured herself coffee and they sat beside each other on the sofa, Adam's arm around his wife.

Then, Adam told the story of Salvation Soll.

Ten years ago Adam was living with his first wife, Reeva, in an oversized Colonial two blocks from downtown. They were both real estate brokers. They met two days before Christmas a year earlier.

Adam's boss, Hank "Herc" Bowman, of Bowman's Real Estate, introduced Reeva to Adam at the office Christmas party.

Adam shook her hand, looked into her eyes, and felt a euphoria he had not felt since his first date with Cindy Civetti from high school.

"Reeva's coming to work for us after the holidays," Herc said, a glass of Scotch in his hand. "Thought I'd let her learn the lay of the land during this down time." Herc owned a gym and lifted weights there every morning, standing in front of his closest friend, the mirror, and always walked with his chest puffed out. He winked at Adam. Herc winked a lot.

At the party that afternoon, after three beers, Adam, trembling with anticipation and guilt – Herc Bowman forbade interoffice dating, which was ironic since he tried to bed every female broker in town – asked Cindy if she would like to "get coffee sometime."

"How about dinner?" she said. "My treat."

The following October, on a warm Saturday at dusk, Adam and Reeva got married on the beach – specifically, Herc's beach; he owned a house overlooking Vineyard Sound. They danced on the huge deck, got drunk and slept in the upstairs bedroom (Herc left for the night with one of Reeva's friends).

Adam was happier than he had ever been and became Falmouth's top-selling broker at age 28. Soon, assumed Adam, he and Reeva, would quit working for the loathsome swine Bowman and open their own real estate brokerage. It was Adam's idea of a perfect life, albeit one only a workaholic could appreciate.

It was Dec. 22, the one-year anniversary of their meeting, when Adam told Reeva he was going to deliver presents to a few friends. Reeva said she had to finish her Christmas shopping. Adam kissed her and said he'd take care of dinner.

Adam did not want to, but felt obligated to buy Herc a gift. He picked up a bottle of 12-year-old Scotch and drove to his boss's house.

Reeva's Mercedes was in the driveway.

"She must be doing the same thing I'm doing," thought Adam until he looked through the front door and saw Herc kissing Reeva's neck, standing there in her red bra, panties, garter belt and high heels.

Adam grabbed a snow shovel off the porch, smashed the window, unlocked the door and rushed into the house. He charged at Herc, threw a punch and Herc caught it like a baseball. He lifted Adam, leaving him dangling like a lobster in the supermarket seafood guy's hand.

Then Adam kicked Herc in the crotch.

That night, when Reeva left with some clothing, her briefcase, makeup and a hairdryer, Adam threw the Christmas tree in the yard and drank most of the 12-year-old Scotch.

At 4 a.m., he started walking in the cold.

He went down Main Street half a mile, turned right and walked into the Wal-Mart parking lot, which was brightly lit. First, Adam heard the singing. Then, he saw the man sitting in a chair and playing guitar.

When Adam got close to the singer, he saw a plaque leaning against an open guitar case. It said: "Blessed are the peacemakers; for they shall be called the children of God."

Still a bit drunk, Adam found himself singing. The song was "I Ain't Got No Home in This World Anymore" by Woody Guthrie. When the man finished the song – "Oh, the gamblin' man is rich an' the workin' man is poor. And I ain't got no home in this world anymore" – Adam clapped.

"Thank you kindly," the man said.

He wore a black fedora with a red feather and a long black coat, jeans and cowboy boots. Adam thought his clothes were too clean and his face was too clean-shaven for him to be homeless.

The man stood, placed his guitar on the chair seat and offered Adam his hand. Adam shook it. "Solomon," he said. "They call me Salvation Soll."

"Adam Delmonico. You have a very good voice. But Woody Guthrie isn't exactly Christmas music, Soll."

"Figure people get enough of that so-called Christmas music inside the stores," Soll said. "Why not give them a break."

"I like that," Adam said and asked Soll if he knew another Guthrie song, "Jesus Christ," and Soll said he did. He started singing:

Jesus Christ was a man who traveled through the land
Hard working man and brave
He said to the rich, "Give your goods to the poor."
So they laid Jesus Christ in his grave.

After the song Adam asked Soll where he came from and Soll answered, "I'm from all over."

"Been traveling, have you?" Adam said.

"You could say that," Soll said.

"What brings you to Cape Cod?"

Soll pointed to a small camper that looked brand new. "Go wherever I'm needed."

"Whoever is in need of salvation?"

Soll smiled. "If the shoe fits."

"You have family?" Adam asked.

"Well, daddy's a brimstone, baritone anti-cyclone rolling stone preacher from the east."

Adam answered: "He says, 'Dethrone the dictaphone, hit it in its funny bone, that's where they expect it least. Bruce Springsteen lyrics."

"You got me," Soll said, and Adam decided right then he liked this man.

Adam stayed listening to Soll singing and playing until the store opened and customers tossed money into Soll's guitar case.

When Adam started walking home, he realized he no longer felt depressed. But he was still angry. Mosty angry at Herc. "Maybe I'll burn down his gym," Adam thought.

After a few hours of sleep that night Adam went for a walk to WalMart. It was Christmas Eve morning. Adam did not know where Reeva was and he did not care. He decided he was not going to forgive her. He would divorce her, sell the house and start his own business. And maybe murder Herc; he fantasized about shooting him inside the gym while he did curls.

At Wal-Mart, Adam was happy to see Soll up and singing some Bob Dylan at 5 a.m. His audience was a driver in his taxi cab who sipped coffee and read a newspaper.

Adam noticed a second chair beside Soll, who launched into his next song, "Reason to Believe."

…knowing that you lied straight-faced while I cried; still I look to find a reason to believe…

When he finished, he set down the guitar in the case. "Have a seat in my office," Soll said. "Coffee?"

"Sure."

Soll poured coffee from a Thermos into mugs.

"So," Soll said. "I'm feeling some anger emanating from you. Some dangerous anger. Painful and dangerous."

"As a matter of fact," Adam began and he went on to tell Soll what had happened two days prior. He told Soll he was rife with resentment, how he could not imagine hating Herc more than he did before he caught him with his wife, but he did. Adam was afraid of what he would do next time he encountered Henry Bowman, egotistical Realtor scoundrel.

"You may want to take heed of the Beatitude there by my guitar case," Soll said. "To the casual observer, it seems a mere conventional religious generalization. It isn't. This is Jesus teaching us the invaluable lesson in the art of prayer. And prayer is the only thing that changes your character. Something that would do you a world of good."

"I'm listening," said Adam.

"A change in character is an essential change. When it happens, you become a different person and from then on, you act in a different way from the way you used to act when you did not pray. You want a dramatic change in your character? Do you want your outlook and habits to change?"

"Do I want to be reborn, as it were?"

"Exactly."

"I'm willing to try. If it enables me to shake this anger and desire for revenge."

"Serenity will come a little at a time if you continue to pray and feel a presence of God," Soll said. "Eventually you will know a real soul peace. You will overcome any difficulties."

"And I'll be a peace maker?"

"Yes, those who attain this true serenity, or peace, are the peace makers Jesus spoke of in the Beatitude."

So, one day Adam was an angry, lonely soul; the next day he was trying to understand the power of prayer.

On the walk home, he started talking to God. That night just before going to bed, he spoke to God again. And he slept better than he had in years.

On Christmas morning, after prayer, Adam went walking. To his surprise and relief, Soll's camper was still parked in the WalMart . Soll sat beside it singing, "Mothers Don't Let Your Babies Grow Up to be Cowboys."

"Merry Christmas," Soll said when he finished singing.

"Merry Christmas, Soll. Thought you'd be somewhere with someone."

"Nope. Just waiting on you. Come on inside."

Adam and Soll sat inside the camper. "Have some spiked 'nog?" Soll said, pouring himself egg nog and Southern Comfort. "It's not 5 a.m. in New Zealand."

"Why not?" Adam said.

They drank and talked.

Mostly, Soll explained the rest of the Beatitudes to Adam. "You learn what Jesus was talking about during the Sermon on the Mount, you will be a new man. A man with no anger. A man at peace."

Adam asked Soll if he had family or friends to be with; Soll said, "Sure, but this is more important."

"Bless you," Adam said. He gave Soll his business card. "Call if you're ever this way again," he said.

The next day Soll's camper was still in the lot. But Adam could not find Soll.

By springtime, Adam was again the top seller among brokers in town. He started Delmonico Real Estate.

When he saw Reeva and Herc walk in at one of his open houses, he silently asked God for peace and wisdom and felt calm. "Maybe this is what it feels like to be a child of God," he thought.

One year after meeting Salvation Soll, one solid year of prayer later, Adam received a text message that said:

am in key west all is well merry xmas. soll

Adam felt relieved and was glad he had given Soll his business card.

At 3 the next morning Adam lept out of bed. "Why not?" he said.

He went to sit at his laptop and began searching for a Key West itinerary. He got a flight for Dec. 28 – Boston to Chicago to Miami and on to Key West aboard one of those – shudder -- tiny planes.

In Key West, Adam walked for two days searching for Soll. Surely he would be someplace on Duval Street sipping a drink or by the water playing his guitar (or maybe outside Hemmingway's house).

Adam repeatedly sent text messages and voice mail to Soll. No response.

He headed back home New Year's Eve morning. The flight was at 8 a.m. Adam was too disappointed to spend New Year's Eve alone in Key West.

On the plane at Key West Airport, Adam was reading *Rolling Stone*, trying to keep his mind off being in such a tiny plane bound for Miami, when he heard a woman's voice say, "Excuse me."

He looked up. His heart skipped. Adam stood and let the woman get to her seat right beside him.

"Happy New Year," she said.

"God, give me the right words," Adam said to himself, and began talking to the woman. He felt calm. He also decided he now knew what love at first sight felt like.

"I'm Samaria," the woman said. "My mother thumbed through the Bible a lot when she was pregnant. My brothers are named Isaiah and Solomon."

(Each year during Adam's telling of the story, Jake would explain: After King Solomon's death about 2900 years ago, the Kingdom of Israel split into two halves. The southern half was called Judah. The northern half, which continued to be called Israel, designated the city of Samaria to be its new capitol, rather than Jerusalem, which was located in Judah. The city of Samaria is located on a hill about 35 miles north of Jerusalem.)

When the plane shimmied and shook, Sam grabbed Adam's hand. The euphoria he felt when he met Reeva? That was nothing compared to this.

When Adam asked where she was headed, Samaria said, "You won't believe this. But I'm going to go retrieve my brother, Soll's camper in Fairhaven."

"Could this be possible?" Adam said.

"What's that?" Sam said.

"Is your brother Salvation Soll? Tall, lanky guy with long hair? Plays guitar?"

"Salvation Soll, Seaside Soll, Sayonara Soll, Psycho Soll…he's had a very colorful life. How do you know him?"

Adam told Sam about their meeting, told her everything.

Samaria and Solomon rented out jet skis at Key West. Each year around Christmas, Soll hits the road in his camper and stays at a Wal-Mart. Sam flies to that city and drives back. "I make a vacation out of it," she said. "I spend the night wherever I feel like, do some sightseeing."

"You don't have to take this bus. I can drive you to Fairhaven on the way to the Cape," Adam said. "My car is at Logan."

By the time they arrived in Fairhaven, Adam was giddy, ready to ask Sam to marry him.

Instead, he asked her if she wanted some company on the drive back to Key West; she said she'd love it. She followed Adam in the camper. They shopped for groceries and cooked dinner together at Adam's house. They talked and laughed until midnight. The next morning they left for the trip south.

Two weeks later, Adam flew back home. He spoke to Sam every day by phone. When Adam's divorce was final and his house sold, Sam flew up and they found a new home together; Sam always wanted to live on the Cape.

A Justice of the Peace married them Dec. 22 – in the Wal-Mart parking lot. "Where else would be more significant?" Sam asked Adam.

Soll had driven up in the camper. When the ceremony, witnessed by a few friends plus Jake and Joshua finished, Soll grabbed his guitar and sang "Have Yourself A Merry Little Christmas."

The curious, delighted crowd of about 200 watching the wedding began singing loudly. Then, everyone clapped.

Years later, when Jake and Joshua were 14 and 16 respectively, they still ate Christmas Eve pizza and still sat by the tree waiting for their dad to tell the story of their Uncle Soll, whom they never met.

It was the year the Delmonicos added to their Christmas Eve tradition. "Come on, let's do it," Jake said when his father finished the story.

"But we were going to watch White Christmas?" Adam said.

"Yawn," Jake said.

"Yeah, yawn," said Joshua.

"The store will be closed in a half hour," Sam said. "No one will be there."

"Mom," said Jake. "It's 2013, an apex of consumerism. It's WalMart. People will be there."

And so they went.

At the Wal-Mart entrance, 20 minutes before closing, Adam, Sam, Jake and Josh sang "Have Yourself A Merry Little

Christmas," and as shoppers exited the store, they stopped. They sang. They hugged.

"Merry Christmas," Jake and Josh called out.

"Merry Christmas," came the reply from so many shoppers.

Adam looked up at the stars. "Thank you, God," he said.

"Thank you, Soll," Adam and his wife said.

DANCING NAKED

SMACKWATER JACK

Let's begin here, San Luis, a small town in deep south-central Colorado. I camped just outside of town in my trailer. There isn't much here . . . the R&R Market, the town courthouse, Museum and Cultural Center, The San Luis Motel, a Mexican restaurant and a couple of breakfast places. This is an old town; it feels old, spent with eyes half-closed. San Luis is, in fact, the oldest town in Colorado. June 21, 1851 . . . a date that is still celebrated at the annual Fiesta de San Luis. It feels Latino. You know? Citizens walk the streets slowly looking for someplace to sit. They have black satin hair with skin like worn saddles. There is music here, from way down the street, off in time. Mariachis. Music—like old stories—that never die.

I'm trying to find a woman. Her name is Virginia Dale. Or Maria Virginia Dale? Or Virginia Ramos? Or Maria Ramos? She's dead now, died around 1900 at 70 years of age after three chaotic marriages. Someone said she died in Missouri. I have had a wild virtual love affair with this woman since I first read about her in my great grandfather's trail diary. He was a Pony Express rider out here. George Scovell was his name. He didn't say much about her, only "an exotic woman with a challenging look." Then he added, "It was said there was hardly a jacket she could fasten around her "bosom." I was hooked. Other descriptions of this woman were, she was "voluptuous and lively" . . . "a woman of handsome features even though she weighed in at 160 pounds on a very tall frame." Also "sour-countenanced, and heavy-haunched". She had "long dark curls that fell to her shoulders." Many reported that she was an expert shot, an expert rider, a graceful dancer and could be "the most charming woman in the West." Yet she had "a questionable reputation." She got her start here in San Luis, I am told . . .in a hoochie-coochie house. The town is rife with these rumors. . . rumors that give her a richness.

She married Joseph Alfred Slade, also known as "Mad Jack." He lived here in the late 1850's. A lot has been written about this enigmatic man. "A kind gentleman, disarming." Mark Twain wrote about him in <u>Roughing It</u>. Said he was "a pleasant person, friendly and gentle-spoken." My great grandfather described him as, ". . . quite a nice fellow but I heard gruesome stories about his temper.

"Mr. Slade carries a human ear on his watch fob."

Clearly there was another side of Jack Slade; the Mad Jack side . . . violent, self-centered, ruthless, quick tempered. When he was drinking he became totally out of control and has been chronicled as one of the craziest, most impulsive gunmen in the West.

DANCING NAKED

I have heard so many stories about the "Slades" that I finally sorted out what I wanted to believe. That's what happens in history. We read and research and build a human profile which morphs into a real person in our minds with a personality that we give them. On the way we develop personal feelings about that character.

So, I like Jack Slade. Because of my great grandfather I know a lot about him. More than most people and historians. Jack. Fun, a good friend but if you ever crossed him he'd kill you. I covet his wife but that would definitely get me killed.

He first killed a man when he was 14. The guy he killed was an old man who berated him—screamed and yelled. Wouldn't stop—until young Jack had had enough. He picked up a big rock and slammed the old man in the head . . . several times, the story goes. His parents whisked him away by enlisting him in the army. He served in the Mexican War, and fought in the battle of Resaca de la Palma in Brownsville, Texas. One of the bloodiest hand-to-hand, face-to-face battles of any war. Slade survived. He was 17. He remembered his age, because that was the number of men he had killed when he was discharged. Sixteen valid enemies and one old son-of-a-bitch.

Jack Slade was a short little guy with tough, hard-carved features. A swagger that took over a bar room, and an apparent temper with no limits. He had two hollow legs for whiskey. In 1845 in a crowded bar near Amarillo, Texas, late at night and drunk, he shot Enrique Cardoza in the forehead. From "less than a foot in distance" he did it because the arrogant Cardoza dared him. Then he apologized to Cardoza's friends for "messing up the place." He left town, slowly on horseback, finger on his trigger, very aware of his back.

Back to San Luis. It's like many other old western towns, except it is filled with la musica . . . that Latino romance thing. A permanence. A feeling, an emotion that will never go away. Mexicanos say, la musica que llego para quedarse. The music that remains forever. There is a certain swoon here like a sudden remembrance of soft, eye-watery sex. Of love. Amor. San Luis is where Jack Slade met and married Virginia Dale. He called her Molly. She would remain with him for the rest of his life.

Romance prevails. I long to know this woman. What does she look like? A writer by the name of Dan Rottenberg posted a photograph of a single-eyebrowed, flat-chested woman with a big nose, wearing a bustle (or are those the heavy haunches?). He said it was a photograph of Virginia Dale.

I prefer to believe she looked like Dorothy Malone who played her in the 1953 movie Jack Slade.

Most of the facts about Virginia reveal a fascinating woman who stood by her man. Protective, loving yet harsh. With a husband like Jack, she had to be harsh, controlling and literally as dangerous as he was. It is reported that she possessed a rather unlovely character and was forever interfering in her husband's business. In fact, a lot of their troubles seem to have originated with her. If ever there was a woman who could drive her husband to drink, it was said to be Virginia Dale. But oh how Jack loved her. And oh how he loved his whiskey.

Jack and Molly left San Luis around 1850 and spent the next few years in the Front Range of Colorado. He captained wagon trains and became known as a tough taskmaster and very efficient as long as he was sober.

Then they became inexorably linked to a small town in the far north east corner of the state, called Julesburg. This was Jules Beni's town. So vain he was that he named it after himself. He settled there in 1854 after several years as a dishonest trapper selling pelts, fingers, blond scalps and genitalia. By everyone's account—who ever knew him or heard of him—Jules Beni was a liar, a crook and a murderer. Because of Julesburg's location it was perfect for a stage and mail stop . . . or hold up.

In 1858 Jack Slade became a superintendent for the Central Overland California and Pikes Peak Express Company and was hired to track down horse thieves. Jules Beni was one of them. Slade caught up with him at Julesburg, but in the ensuing affray Slade was out-gunned. Everybody thought that he was dead. Several angry townsfolk chased Beni out of Julesburg, but when they returned they found Slade struggling to his feet and anxious to return to his home to recover.

Virginia, it seems, was furious that anyone would out-gun her man. She knew that Jack was a kill-er, not a kill-ee. As she nursed him back, they planned Jack's revenge, feeding the anger each day like picking a scab on a hot wound.

Beni continued to steal horses from the Pike's Peak Express Company and brag about shooting Slade. He decided to ambush Slade and finish what he started. Slade found out about it from a prostitute whom Beni had abused . . . left her tied to a 4-poster in the local hotel, a cocked pistol between her legs.

Along with some of his cowboys, and a well-armed Virginia . . . plus the prostitute, they surprised Beni. The entourage was so furious at Beni, they heatedly argued who would do him in. No one ever thought of taking him to the proper authorities for trial. Slade won—gun drawn—and tied Beni to a fencepost, then shot him slowly "from the groin area up." Then he cut off Beni's ears and headed to Julesburg. One would be nailed to a fencepost on the outskirts of town, the other, Jack made into a watch fob. . .the one my great grandfather saw.

I met an old farmer in Julesburg by the name of Othie. Never learned his last name. He used to sell baby pigs' ears on key chains as souvenirs—said they were Beni's ears. He told me he made a fortune, as he stood there with an empty wallet next to his beat up and rusted pickup. There must have been an era of earless pigs that no one has recounted.

It was at that point in Virginia and Jack's life that Slade totally gave in to booze, shooting and beating people indiscriminately. He built his own town in north central Colorado and named it after his wife. Virginia Dale. It's still there, a tiny unincorporated town located in the foothills of the Rocky Mountains on U.S. Highway 287. She still stood by her man. Good for Virginia. But Jack was too far gone to change.

Eventually Slade ran afoul of every aspect of the law. He was hanged in 1864. A neighbor told Virginia they had captured Jack and she took off after them but arrived too late. She found his body in a nearby store, the noose still around his neck. The town breathed a sigh of relief and built a coffin for him. Virginia insisted on a tin lining for the coffin . . . and a keg of whiskey which she poured in to preserve his remains. The coffin, the body, and the whiskey lay in her bedroom for several months. Then, strangely, she had his pickled remains sent to the authorities in Salt Lake City, explaining that she would notify the legal system as to what should be done with them.

Virginia Dale never claimed his remains.

His gravestone is in Salt Lake City.

She moved back to their ranch at Virginia Dale and had a short-lived marriage to Jack's best friend. Much later in life and far away from Virginia Dale she married briefly once again. The ranch is long gone. The Virginia Dale Café is closed—the Abbey of St. Walburg, a Benedictine order of nuns ironically has made this their home. Why?

So I sit here in her town in my pickup, computer in my lap, in the parking lot of the now defunct Virginia Dale Café. <u>Smackwater Jack</u> plays on my ipad.

"You can't talk to a man with a shotgun in his hand . . . You can't talk to a man when he don't wanna understand."

"Ahh Molly," I'm sure he would say.

DANCING NAKED

THE CRYSTAL CHRONICLES

One of my earliest memories of Atlantis was of a gigantic Crystal sitting on a platform in the middle of a very large room, much like a laboratory. A room that would house a powerful telescope with an aperture in the roof to emit light and to allow the rays of the Crystal to be focused out through the opening. The walls of this vast room were inlaid with smaller crystals of every shape and composition. They were purposely placed in sacred, geometric patterns, to enhance the Crystal's force. As sunlight streamed into the room through that same aperture in the roof, each of these geometric shapes would ignite. They d send lazar light beams of energy into the Crystal to be stored, and used as trans-dimensional magnetic energy facilitators.

Driven into hyper-waves, her force was inter-galactic. Her emissions were beyond time, allowing instant communication across the universe. When mis-aligned, her rays would and could emit random scalar waves.

The Crystal's physical appearance was a clouded, somewhat pink hue at her enormous base, transforming into a clear translucent spectrum midway to the peak of her points. She measured 30 cubits around her base, was 45 cubits tall, and dwarfed all of the tallest associates who worked within the chamber.

This Crystal's main purpose was that of transmitter for sending and receiving data from Atlantis to her Mother Colony in a Universe in the midst of the Pleiades group.

Carefully guarded, the Crystal had only a select few around her at any given time. I was the only High Priestess chosen to have any contact with her, and that was minimal, which is why I cherished what time I was allowed to spend there.

She was such an ancient soul, only we knew that she had been sent to Atlantis by the Architect of Cosmic Destiny. She had shared that secret with me one day as we sat and communed. No other soul knew.

This was not all she shared. Other information that I am certain was never meant for my ears. Why did she choose me? I believed that she was lonely, missed her Mother Colony and her connections there. All of her associates here on Atlantis were self-centered, greedy and only used her as a means to gain power. They never once considered her as a living, breathing entity. To me, she was my mentor, my teacher, my Master, and I adored her!

A majority of my time was spent in the Blue Therapeutic Healing Chamber in a building adjacent to the one that housed the Crystal. This room was home to me, having spent most of my childhood there with my Mother, a High Priestess and Teacher at the neighboring Atlantis Academy. My Father was also a Professor and Teacher there.

The chamber was changeless, with its walls covered in lapis lazuli and reflecting the facets of the metal, Iron Pyrite, giving the room a profound healing eminence. In the center of the room stood a chair, constructed of clear Lucite that facilitated the healings. It appeared to be floating but was instead, held in place with the energy emitted from the stones in the walls and ultimately, the force from the Crystal. This seat could be adjusted with simple hand movements, and made to move higher or lower depending on the need of the person receiving the healing matrix beams of energy.

On shelves placed around the room were tuning forks constructed of precious metals that created ethereal sounds when struck in a certain way. Set upon, the activator; that sound resonating throughout the room and into the Universe beyond. Other shelves held drums, horns, stringed instruments, and the exquisite Angelic harps, which, when laid upon the body of a person and strummed gently, connected them to the Celestial Music of the Spheres.

On the far wall, just beyond the shelves was another doorway. This one gave entrance to the Rejuvenation Chamber, which was guarded closely by the Emperor's personal soldiers. The use of the chamber was only for those who had proven their worth and their loyalty to the Emperor. This gift was only bestowed once during a lifetime, expanding their current life span an additional two hundred years. I, Silesia, was entrusted to keep watch over these soldiers and no one else. I was the only High Priestess that had the knowledge and proficiency to prepare those entering the chamber and to embrace them when they emerged.

I arose this day with much joy and happiness! This day was my time with my beloved Crystal. As I was preparing myself for this visit, the Government Officials sent a messenger summoning me to appear before them. 'They had some mission for me to undertake' was the communication brought to me by the small but adorable Lemurian slave. Shielding his eyes and looking down at his feet, he cleared his vocals to deliver the short but succinct summons. I rewarded him with several sweet meats and almonds which he hastily placed in his pocket. He bowed, his curly head almost bumping the floor.

Extremely wary, I wondered what they wanted this time. I had been summoned in the past, and I knew what to say and how to act to hide my true feelings. This summons was most intriguing.

*

"They certainly cannot expect me to act the same. It was extremely difficult to keep my expression bland and non-committal. My beloved Crystal, how can I tell her?" Agitated, I left the Government Council Offices and crossed the central courtyard.

As I entered the building that housed the Crystal, my steps lagged. I walked slowly into the chamber. There she sat, in total bliss, unaware of what they had planned for her. She began to glow in greeting and I sent my Heart Greeting to her. Pushing energy from my heart center to hers, her glow increased.

"You are troubled my dearest child?" she began.

"Yes, I am and it concerns you!" I sighed deeply and sat on her platform so that I could touch her.

"I am aware. I know what they are planning to order me to do."

"But, you cannot," I protested.

"I must do as they command."

"It will destroy you!"

"Of that I am aware."

I placed both hands on her Heart Center and felt her warmth emanating through my hands into my body.

"I will not let you." I said, "There must be some way to stop this greed, this insane lust for power." I crumpled against her in uncontrollable tears.

"You must not allow yourself to become immersed in your emotions. They will read that in you. There are eyes and ears everywhere. Even as we speak, they are watching, although they do not understand the exchange we are having. Calm yourself and release your emotions. Assist me to find a different way to handle this. They are human and so are you, but their views are different from ours, so, I need you to guide me through this."

I raised my head and looked at her. "You will use the scalar energy?"

"You read my thoughts. That is good."

"Can they also read your thoughts?"

"No, it is not allowed. That is why you have been chosen to carry this message to me. You are their only entry to me."

"What must I do?"

"Two different approaches, I believe we must take. First, you will carry back a message telling them that I must not do what they plan. The Mother Colony will not sanction it. It will bring massive destruction upon Atlantis. The entire city and kingdom will be at risk."

"This is the message that you wish me to carry to them?"

"Yes."

"But they will not listen to me. The Annanuki will laugh at this and throw it off as some raving dog."

"Yes, that is the plan."

"I don't understand."

"They will not listen; they will go ahead and set in motion their plan. That will allow me to shift into scalar energy."

"Is that not dangerous?"

"Yes, but to get me to that point, this must be the pathway!"

"What does Mother Colony say about this?"

"They are all in accord!"

"There must be more to the plan than this. Are you hiding something from me?"

"I said two parts, remember? That's the first part. This will give you time to alert certain residents of Atlantis; those that you feel must leave, and start that in motion. Your Mother and Father must be among those to evacuate the city."

"Adonais will be of great assistance. We have spoken of this many times, and he has the support of the Warriors and the Inner Guards. What of the Emperor? Is he to be included?"

"No!"

"Why?"

"He is weak and not worthy of escape. He must stay and hold fast to the thoughts and beliefs the Annanuki have fed him. The power, lust and gold are to stay here with him."

"What will happen to Atlantis?"

"First, you will feel the trembling of the Earth as the scalar waves set the plan into motion. The quakes will begin throughout the entire kingdom and chaos will ensue. As that activates, you will have time to gather together and leave Atlantis. Most of you will travel to other colonies that are scattered in numerous locations all over the planet.

"As the tremors and quakes continue in intensity, a mighty wave will cover all of her lands and she will sink into the Atlantic. I will slide into the ocean with her to sit on the bottom and carry on my purpose once more. This time I will be free of human interference. The Mother Colony is in accord. It was predicted that Atlantis would thrive as an ancient culture unsurpassed by no other, but each time it was swallowed up by the greed, lust and power of the ruling governments. In this last unpleasant incident, there is no forgiveness. Atlantis cannot be rescued. This time, its entire civilization and all of her cultures must remain safely concealed in the depths of the ocean until mankind can arise to the nobleness of its societies, its dignity, and its morality."

"You will be safe?"

"Yes, I will be safe and someday I will be re-discovered, but not until the human race is ready to use my powers for the good of humanity and not for their own personal greed and gain."

"I will carry your message. I shall miss you, dear Teacher."

"We will always be connected; neither distance nor time will exist."

"Heart Love, my beloved Crystal."

"Heart Love, my dearest Silesia."

DANCING NAKED

Authors Notes:

Where was Atlantis? No one has really conclusively proven that it was anywhere. Plato describes it in depth in his <u>Timaeus</u> and <u>Critias</u> Dialogues and over the centuries, men have searched for it diligently. Where was its exact location? I believe it was in the middle of what is now the Atlantic Ocean which would coincide with the Edgar Cayce readings. Many of his readings have stated it was the bridge between the continents and this also corresponds with Plato's description.

My Guides stated that it had three cataclysmic events. The first was several minor earthquakes and fire. The second was an intense volcanic eruption. Each time Atlantis re-surfaced after each of those two catastrophes to grow even stronger but the third time, the destruction was complete. It was destroyed forever by numerous earthquakes and several enormous waves.

Why was it destroyed? There are many theories. The ones that stand out in the Edgar Cayce readings, Plato's account and the information that has come from other Spirit Guides, is that the High Officials of Atlantis were becoming corrupt with greed, avarice and the ill-use of their power. They no longer honored their Galactic Connections or kept the spiritual association that Atlantis was originally founded upon. They no longer cared for the needs of the people. Their only concern was their individual lust for power and the wealth that it brought to them.

The Annanuki that are mentioned in the story were the basic cause of the corruption, turning the heads and minds of the High Officials with rewards of political positions and riches, buying their loyalty and their very Souls.

Other students of Atlantean lore speculate that Atlantis was destroyed by other world beings, by Aliens from other Galactic Systems or even more distressing, by their own Mother Colony.

It is alleged by some that the Crystal was and still is a gigantic transmitter for communication between Earth and the Mother Colony. It is also supposed that the Earth's Moon is a satellite that connects Earth to her Galactic Family.

The Bermuda Triangle, perpetually a mystery to many and certainly something to be considered, is also theoretically believed to be a Stargate,. A Portal, a Vortex, where the Atlantean Crystal remains buried deeply in the bottom of the sands of the ocean. This enables her to maintain her established connections with her Mother Colony somewhere within the Pleiades Star System.

The Islands of Bimini and the Bahamas are a few of the ancient vestiges of this once great society and culture.

Truth of Fiction??? That decision is yours to make.

DANCING NAKED

ELEANOR

Fine, I understand
Okay with me, if that's the plan
You can take the stereo, the TV and the video,
The bed, the sheets and pillows,
Before you go.
But for now, unlock the door
What are we doin' all this for?
Let me make you **dinner** *one last time*
Then you'll go your way, and I'll go mine.

And I won't call you baby, anymore
Won't call you baby like I did before
Won't call you baby, anymore
Eleanor
 ---- *Low Millions*

My mornings were perfect. I would walk into the Byrds' Song café in Woods Hole where May Byrd serves her homemade English scones topped with whipped cream and strawberry jam, read Lenny Byrd's daily music quiz question on the white board and order a spicy, double-Mexican, mocha latte.

The regulars might be singing to music from Lenny's vast collection.

One winter morning they sang a verse of Paul Simon's "I Am a Rock."

…I have my books and my poetry to protect me
I am shielded in my armor, hiding in my room, safe within my

womb

I touch no one and no one touches me…

They belted out the chorus with conviction:

I am a rock, I am an island…

After Harris and I had one of our fights, there I was in line listening to Bono of U2 singing "I can't live with or without you" and I had to smile because that was how it was with Harris and me.

But the best part of the morning was not the music, food or coffee. The best part was Lily.

She and I usually sat at the small table by the vintage Wurlitzer, which didn't work, but Lenny kept it because it played one song, B13, "You Really Got Me" by his beloved Kinks. Plus, he said, "a lot of my oldest friends are inside that jukebox."

Lily always smiled when she saw me, closed the book she was reading or her lap top and said, "Eleanor, how are you? Fantastic morning isn't it?" in her Kathleen-Turner-in-Body-Heat voice. Her hair was Japanese maple red and the shade changed depending on the light. At first Lily's overwhelming beauty made me feel self-conscious. I spent no time on my mousey blond hair, was in my work jeans and shirt, pruning shears on my hip. Looking at Lily was like staring at a painting you did not believe someone's hands actually created.

From our first meeting on, we confided in one another like we were already close friends.

We talked through winter, until early spring.

There always was music to divert us from life's ponderousness and give us a reason to pass more time in this fantasy of a café – though the trivial invariably found its way back to the confessional. Conversing with her was like sailing off Woods Hole: in a minute there would be some serious waters.

One morning we might debate singers -- was Paul Rogers better than Robert Plant? -- or drummers -- Ginger Baker or Keith Moon and can you name the drummer for the Barracudas? Then, out of the blue, I would say, "What's your all-time favorite opening lyrics to a blues song?"

"They call it stormy Monday but Tuesday's just as bad," Lily said in a snap. "The B.B. King version, of course. Now, you. What was the worst song of the '80s?"

"Easy. 'Let's Get Physical,' Olivia Newton John. What's your choice?"

"Anything by the band Journey."

"You know their song 'In Your Arms?' My husband and I danced to it at our wedding," I said, no longer jocular. "Mitch sang the words in my ear."

In my mind's eye it was six years ago and I was back on the dance floor at the Rip Tide in Chatham, no shoes, pressed to Mitch, smell of cologne and beer and perspiration. Me wanting to shout at the strangers in the pub, "This is it. This is who you marry, this is the feeling you never thought you'd feel." Mitch telling the DJ to play our favorite Dylan love song, "Love Minus Zero/No Limit," us singing, tears in my eyes…

My love she speaks like silence
Without ideals or violence
She doesn't have to say she's faithful
Yet she's true, like ice, like fire…

"I'm sorry," Lily said. "I never would have mentioned Journey if I'd known."

"No, that's fine. You triggered a cherished memory."

After some silence, I told Lily how Mitch died. Just after he opened the driver's side rear door and slid his banjo onto the back, a drunken driver slammed into the door and took it and Mitch with him. Mitch's best friend, Jack, was inside talking to the owner. They played in a Dixieland band, with Jack on piano.

I smiled remembering their valiant attempts at playing Pig Ankle Rag and Dill Pickle Rag. He was just putting his banjo in the car. Then he was gone.

"That's how I met Mitch," I told Lily through tears, "at one of his gigs down in Chatham. He sat at the next table during a break. He smiled and I initiated our conversation with such gems as, 'Banjo is a really hard instrument, isn't it?'

"The next week he sat beside me and I'd meet him there every week. A few months later I moved into his tiny apartment in this rundown house. He had a small landscaping business, 15 or 20 clients. I had studied horticulture at the vocational school and was working at a nursery and part-time at a bank. I quit both jobs and went to work with Mitch. I planted and weeded and helped him rake; he mowed and pruned – everything else. The best spring, summer and fall of my life. We got married the next spring and a year later, nearly to the day, he died. I am so glad we worked together – all those days spent with my best friend."

I looked away. In my mind's eye, I was in bed, entwined with Mitch just before sunrise, him sticking his hand through my t-shirt sleeve, "Here's the Bourne Bridge, now let's go down to P-Town…"

Lily kept her hand on mine for a long time.

Until an old-timer two tables away said something about pygmy monkeys and Lily and I laughed hard.

DANCING NAKED

Lily's main influence was impressionist painter Frederick Childe Hassam and she taught students in her studio at the Great Egret Gallery a block from the café. She listened to T Bone Walker, Guitar Slim, Robert Johnson or Sonny Boy Williamson, while paining Cape Cod coastal scenes. She switched to singer Tom Waits for portraits. "His writing helps me see the stories in people's faces," she said.

In spring, when the bluefish and stripers arrive, Lily is often fishing at dawn off Nobska Point in a wet suit. Of course, from the road you can't tell the tall, strong, fisherman is a woman.

One morning Skip Hays, a café regular and avid fisherman, parked his pickup beside a yellow Jeep in the lot at the foot of Nobska Point Lighthouse. He went down to the beach to surf-cast. For several minutes he watched a fisherman below the point. He saw the fisherman go in chest-high for a farther cast, then fight four large stripers and carefully step back to shallow water to kneel, unhook and release the fish.

Skip caught nothing. He went to his pickup, peeled off his waders, got inside and lit a cigarette.

In his side-view mirror he saw the fisherman walking toward the Jeep. He saw it was Lily when she removed her hat and shook her hair down.

Later at the café Skip was behind Lily and me in line. After Naomi waited on Lily and she stepped from the counter with her coffee, she saw Skip. "Nice fishing out there, Baird," he said. "You fish as well as you paint."

"You saw me earlier?"

"Yes, from the beach. Didn't know who it was 'til I was sitting in my pickup in the lot. You put me to shame. Who taught you?"

"What, you don't think a woman can be self-taught?"

In fact, in her teens, Lily devoted countless hours, along with boundless energy and faith to painting and fishing. She said she was like the young blues guitarist who heard Robert Johnson playing bass lines on the low strings, rhythm on the middle ones, lead on the treble strings, thought it inconceivable but kept practicing. That guitarist was Eric Clapton.

"Incidentally, Skip. We still need to get together to finish your portrait," Lily said.

"I've been meaning to, but…"

"Come by the gallery soon. OK?"

"Will do. Take it easy."

Skip smiled, turned and went to his usual seat at a round table by the corner window, reserved for the political junkies. As usual, John the retired teacher was spouting something negative about Obama (John's nickname was Kennedy because he was perpetually running for office in town). As usual, Ed the real estate broker studied his New York Times crossword puzzle. When John stopped to take a breath, Ed said, "Pair of cymbals in a drum kit, five letters."

"Hi-hat," John said. "Give me a tough one."

"OK. Baloney, in Bristol. Four letters. First letter T."

"Tosh."

Ed handed John the puzzle. "Here, you finish it."

Lily liked Skip. He was always a gentleman and the one who berated his cohorts one morning for their vociferous disapproval of gay marriage. When Skip's son, Richard, got sick the previous winter, Lily helped him with medical expenses. Skip, rehabbing from rotator cuff surgery, could not rake for clams, his source of income. And he had alimony payments. Lily gave him a money order, knowing he'd rip up a check. Richard died a week later.

Lily told me she gave money to a few struggling café regulars because, "That's the least I can do with money I didn't have to work for."

She got to know the café owners Lenny and May Byrd when they took her night-school art class. Over lunch one day, May, who started dating Lenny in high school, told Lily about her husband's plan to quit his custodial job at the Oceanographic Institute and open a café. The corner building that used to be a convenient store and deli for decades was still for lease. "Lenny figures business wouldn't dry up because of the ferry terminal and the Oceanographic Institute." May said. "Plus, we'd have our year-'round regulars, hopefully. It's his dream. Making people happy with coffee and music. I told Lenny I'd work there if he stopped smoking. And no Sex Pistols or New York Dolls. He makes me crazy, playing that punky music at home."

Lily insisted on helping get them started. She wrote them a check. "I'll take the money under one condition," Lenny told her. "Let me hang some of your paintings to sell."

"If you let me do a portrait of you and May," Lily said.
"Deal."

"One more thing," Lily said. "No Billy Joel." Lily cringed whenever she heard his music since the night he hit on her at a bar when she was visiting friends in the Hamptons.

"Deal," said Lenny.

DANCING NAKED

The portrait hangs with seven other works by Lily. Despite their deal, once in a while Lenny plays Billy Joel and laughs watching Lily get a bit riled.

On a December morning I stood behind Lily in line. She smiled a hello to Naomi Byrd, who wore a body hugging brown leopard-print dress and emerald-colored scarf. She had a rose-on-barbed-wire tattoo on her right arm, a lotus flower on her left. She was pouring steamed milk and coffees and talking to the other barista, her brother David – no tattoos, several piercings. They had an ongoing debate about the Dead Boys vs. the Ramones.

Lenny appeared when the line stretched past the antique Victor Victrola. Sometimes Lenny asked a music question geared to a regular customer. This one was a nod to Lily:

Who got rained on with his own .38 in a Tom Waits song?
"The usual, Lily?" Naomi said.
"Small Change," Lily said.
"Small change in your order?"
"No." Lily pointed to the quiz question on the white board.
"Oh, right. Small Change. The song. Correctamundo." Naomi rang the bell signaling a winner, then gave Lily her free coffee and scone.

"Love your scarf," Lily said, turned and went to her usual table. Several male heads turned – as usual -- when her tan Tony Lama western boot heels clacked on the wide, worn pine floor boards. Tom Waits's voice, which was coarse enough to sand that floor, came from the speakers.

Small Change got rained on with his own .38
And nobody flinched down by the arcade…

"Sounds like he gargles with gravel," I said to Lily when I sat with her.

"No, Eleanor. Diamonds."

Lily lived near the café on Penzance Point in Woods Hole at the heel of Cape Cod in the guest house beside her parents' estate that faced the ocean. Lily's two sisters lived out of state.

When I asked Lily if she was married, she said, "not conventionally. Jaymes and I have been together 17 years – with a three-year intermission."

"Let me guess," I said. "He's tall, gorgeous and rugged. He wind-surfs and wears flannel shirts and Timberlands untied."

"Jaymes is a woman. It's J-A-Y-M-E-S."

"I'm sorry." I could feel my face redden. Neil Young was singing "Only Love Can Break Your Heart."

"No worries," Lily said. "Actually, you're close to describing the reason for our three-year intermission."

Lily was a descendent of 19th century <u>American Naturalist</u> and <u>Ornithologist</u> Spencer Fullerton Baird, who became interested in maritime research while vacationing with his wife and daughter in Woods Hole, where they settled.

Lily was born Lilith. But she renounced the name as a teenager. Not because it reminded her of Adam's first wife, Lilith, who refused to be subservient and left him, according to Jewish folklore. Because it reminded her of Lilith on the TV show Cheers. And that reminded her of her father. "I don't know if he was in love with Bebe Neuwirth or her snotty TV character," Lily said. "It did not matter. What mattered was father never paid that kind of attention to me."

DANCING NAKED

Creedon Fullerton Baird never doted on his youngest daughter. "He resented me. There were already three girls. He was 40 when I was born and I was his last shot at the boy he wanted so badly," Lily said looking out the window. "Father wanted someone he could groom. A man to reign over his firm and an inheritance one day. And I spent years trying to please him enough to forget his need for a son. For his love, for any form of affection, I would do anything. It was futile. I spent a lot of time in my room with my sister's Sounds of Silence album singing 'I am a Rock.'"

Lily's father, now 81, was recovering from surgery. He needed a stent to open a coronary artery. Following the procedure, he bled into his lungs and required a breathing tube. Lily's mother, despite their imperfect marriage, helped nurse him.

When Lily was growing up, her father worked at his Boston law firm and returned to the Cape weekends. "My sisters were convinced he cheated on mother. He spent two days home with the family and the rest of the week probably in a hotel suite with a woman half his age."

A lot like Elvis, I thought to myself. He had his Memphis girlfriends and his on-the-road women.

On Lily's 21st birthday, a Sunday, over birthday cake and coffee – "Mother always strove for normalcy" -- Lily told her parents she was gay. Her mother embraced her. They wept together.

"My father said, 'What rubbish,'" Lily told me. "He always wore a gray turtleneck sweater to match his combed-back collar-length gray hair, which annoyed me. He stormed from the living room straight to his den to pour a Scotch, put on his half-moon glasses and headphones to listen to Beethoven's Eroica Symphony while he read some Christian philosopher like Niebur or Dostoevsky. With the door closed, of course."

The next weekend he called Lily to the den. He shut the door and they sat on the leather sofa.

"I'll never forget what father said," Lily said. "I understand you have this… illness, Lilith. But there is nothing to worry about. You can be cured. I have found a renowned psychoanalyst who specializes in reparative therapy, through Spencer Hampton from the firm. He has a son who suffered from such an affliction and he's perfectly normal now. Spencer assured me it works for women, too.

"He went to his desk, picked up a pamphlet and handed it to me. It said The Way Back Through Prayer on the cover. My body began to ache with sadness. I did not want any cure. I wanted support. But I did not protest. Maybe now I can please him, I thought. Maybe he will approve of me."

Lily sipped her coffee, forked some jam and scone. "What I should have done was spit in his face," she said. "Tell him how ashamed I was that he was my father. But my self-esteem was circling the drain. I know it's hard to believe a 21-year-old woman, free to go her own way, would agree to such a thing. But I was like my mother. I hungered for affection. That and, I'm embarrassed to say, the security Creedon Baird provided. Money, in other words.

"I never said a word. Just watched him write a check while telling me to never breathe a word of this to a soul, not even mother. I was to tell her that he was sending me to Italy to study Botticelli and da Vinci. A birthday gift. 'If you need anything during your time away,' he said when he handed me the check. Bull. It was hush money.

"A week later, I was at a reparative therapy camp in New York City."

"What if you refused to go?" I asked.

" I knew if I didn't go, I'd be out of the will. And I wanted as much as I could get out of that prick. He threatened my sister, Annie, with that when she started dating a carpenter. She told him to – excuse my language –go fuck himself. Annie is my heroine. She's 12 years my senior and we've always been close. She married Randy and they live in Arizona now."

Lily rose from her chair. "How about another coffee?"

"Sure," I said, welcoming the chance to exhale.

Lily went behind the counter to visit with Lenny and May. They laughed.

When Lily returned, she said Lenny was asking about me. Am I into music? Am I a local gal? Do I know the rules of the music quiz?

"I told him you are an Elvis scholar. Lenny always vets his prospective regulars," Lily said. "You know, if you're going to be family. And you're family now. Lenny's noticed you've been here every day for almost a month and you answered nine questions correctly."

"Hey, ladies," Lenny said, approaching our table.

"Lenny, this is Eleanor," Lily said and Lenny shook my hand. He was wearing a "God Save The Kinks" t-shirt. He was sharp-boned, tall and wiry with hair in an elastic band halfway down his back and piercing summer-ocean-colored eyes. Lily told me he played guitar in a '70s rock band. He quit the night he dropped acid, looked down and couldn't tell what he was holding.

Lily said people still talk about Lenny's performance last summer on his 57th birthday. The previous year he came out singing the Kinks' "Alcohol," waving a beer like Ray Davies used to do on stage. But this time Lenny walked to the piano, played the beautiful opening of REM's "Nightswimming," and sang the song. Several jaws dropped. Then, Lenny stood, turned around, bowed, and went back behind the counter to applause.

Lenny said, "So, you're into Elvis. The early years or the bloated, drugged-up Vegas years?"

"Both," I said. "His life is so fascinating. He was this magnetic, kind, mama's boy and incredibly emotional singer who became so tragic. The vulnerable kid who stood in his driveway signing autographs until his mother called him in for supper became the drug-dependent man who rode his three-wheeler at 2 a.m. in his bathrobe."

"Were you even born when Elvis died?"

"I was 5 in 1977."

"How'd you get into him?"

"I first heard him when my mom played his records, which she got from my grandmother. I danced with them to "Blue Suede Shoes" when I was little; when I was older I got intrigued with his life and started reading. I owe the rest of my music knowledge to my big brother. He gave me his vinyl, his cassettes and CDs. And books."

"An Elvis scholar," Lenny said, his arms folded.

"Just an average student."

Lenny pursed his lips, looked at me hard.

"What were Elvis's parents' names?"

"Come on. Too easy. Gladys and Vernon."

"OK...Who was sleeping in his bed when he died on the bathroom floor?"

"Ginger Alden."

"Woa," Lily said. "Take that, Lenny."

Lenny rubbed his hands together. I felt my cheeks flush.

"Name three of the drugs found in his system when he died."

"Seconal, Placidyl, Valmid."

At the next table, Aidan, a ruddy faced, gray haired man in his 70s, started chanting "Go, go, go" and clapping.

I went. "Elvis's pajama bottoms around his ankles were gold-colored, and the book he had with him explained the correlation between the planets and sexual positions," I said. "He was pronounced dead at 3 p.m. and Colonel Parker wore a baseball cap, seersucker pants and a short-sleeved shirt to the funeral. Would you like the names of the nine pallbearers?"

"No," said Lenny, putting his hands up. "I surrender."

Lily offered me a hand to high-five.

"Lenny, I have one for you," I said. "Why did Ray Davies change Coca-Cola to cherry cola in the song, 'Lola?'

"Come on. Child's play. Because the BBC wouldn't allow songs that named products."

When Lenny left, Lily was still smiling.

I shrugged. "What can I say? I read a lot."

Lily said she needed to get to her gallery to work with a student. When we hugged, I felt something deep down. Lily promised to finish her story the next morning.

When I got to the café at 6:30 the next morning, I knew the quiz question was Lenny's way of letting me know I was officially a regular. He was saluting me:

Why did Elvis start wearing his collar up at concerts?

"To cover up the acne on his neck," I said to Naomi. She didn't have to ask what I was having. She made my spicy Mexican mocha latte and rang the bell. Then she played the Elvis song, "Be My Lucky Charm."

Lily listened to my Elvis impersonation.

Don't want a four leaf clover
Don't want an old horse shoe
Want your kiss 'cause I just can't miss
With a good luck charm like you
Come on and be my little good luck charm…

I anxiously asked Lily to continue with her story.

"The camp," I said. "What was it like?"

"It was surreal," Lily said. "Christian fundamentalist gurus banking on Stockholm syndrome. Nausea-inducing drugs and shock treatment".

"My God. Who was in charge of this camp?".

"The head shrink was Dr. Spaulding. I'll never forget him. He had a mustache and black-rimmed glasses. Looked like Groucho Marx. So, we called him Captain Spaulding."

I laughed. "The Groucho character in Animal Crackers. That's priceless."

Hooray for Captain Spaulding, the African explorer, Lily sang.

"How long were you there?"

"One week. The first few days, I went with the program. The next morning came my catharsis: this is wrong and cruel. Just horrid. Being gay is not wrong, not a choice. This is who I am and who I want to be. My father is the one who is sick.

"I spent the final days trying to convince other campers – as in concentration campers – being gay was not immoral, but it was futile. They wanted to stay. Then, Dr. Spaulding expelled me for insubordination.

"In a way, Eleanor, it was best thing that ever happened to me, because that's where I met Jaymes. She was under the impression she'd leave straight and be back in her parents' and husband's good graces. We were synchronized in coming to our senses. We signed out weeks before we were scheduled to. We even walked out of the place at the same time –that gives me chills, to think of that now. I was immediately struck by her smile when I held the door for her."

They shared a cab. Lily told Jaymes she was headed to the Metropolitan Museum of Art to view its collection of European 19th Century paintings. Jaymes agreed to go. They spent the day trading stories. Jaymes was 24, a massage therapist and was studying to be a yoga instructor.

They ate Carnegie Deli cheesecake and walked miles. Jaymes was flying back home to Taos to tell her husband, sorry, but that therapy thing didn't take. We need a divorce. And Lilly had to face her father.

But both were not expected back to their homes for another three weeks.

"I told Jaymes I had father's money, so we could check into a hotel room and see the city. "Jaymes agreed, to my delight," Lily said.

The mini vacation turned out to be life-changing.

Lily hatched a plan.

"We took the earliest bus back to the Cape, talking non-stop the whole time," Lily said after I bought two more coffees –

this time decaf. "It was a Sunday, so I knew my father would be home. I had called mother and said I made a friend in Rome. We were both throwing coins into the Trevi fountain, it was so romantic, and we're at Logan and I'd like to bring Jaymes home with me. Mother said, 'I'd love to meet the young man. And I'd bet your father would, too.' I told her Jaymes was from Ohio and always wanted to see Cape Cod. I pictured my father calling Spenser Hampton to thank him because his daughter was cured."

Jaymes was not hesitant in joining forces with her new lover, Lily said. "It was like we were feeding off each other's new-found confidence, and trust."

"And after only a few weeks," I said.

"It's hard to explain, Eleanor. How strong the connection was."

They took a bus to Woods Hole from Logan and a short cab ride to the estate.

"Mother greeted us at the door," Lily said. "I introduced Jaymes. Then, I said, 'We've fallen in love.'

'Oh,' is all mother could say and she covered her mouth with her hand. Her face said, 'What on Earth will Creedon do now?'

"Mother ushered us into the living room and asked if we wanted anything to eat or drink. Not until we see father, I told her. I told Jaymes to wait in the living room then went to knock on the den door. Father opened it and I went inside. His headphones and his book were on a butler's table. 'Why, Lilith, how great to see you,' he said. 'Why didn't you call for a lift? Your friend? Is he here?'

"That's when I called to Jaymes. Father, I said, this is Jaymes. We are together. We are a couple. Sit down and listen.

We sat, father in his Queen Ann chair, Jaymes and I on the sofa. Father looked like he had a burglar training a gun on him. He told us to get out, that we disgusted him.

I told him to sit back down and what was going to happen, was that Jaymes and I were staying in the guest house. He told me he was taking me out of the will.

"Forget it, I told him. I said, You will withdraw money from the bank tomorrow morning for this amount -- and I took a pen from his desk and wrote a number on a piece of paper, handed it to him. My father laughed.

Then I said, You will wire that same amount to my account at Peoples Bank in Taos when I call with the information in a month.

Father's face reddened. "I will do no such thing, he said. 'Was extortion your lesbian friend's idea?'

"I told him the alternative was that I would tell mother all about his bimbo dalliances in Boston. I was aware that his prenuptial agreement stipulated in the event of adultery -- mother is a savvy woman – the estate got sold and the adulterer got none of the money. I told him it behooved him to play ball."

"Did you really have proof of his affairs?" I asked Lily.

"When I left the camp, I called Annie," she said. "As I said, we are very close. She told me about the pictures. Father and his girlfriends at the Ritz Carlton. When father said he was dropping her from the will, Annie hired a private detective. That's him at the corner table."

I looked over at the gray-haired man in a blue Polo dress shirt, khakis and tassel loafers, no socks.

"Cazzie. The guy who's always winking at you," I said.

"Now you know why."

"How did you get the pictures? Annie was in Arizona."

"She put copies – this is so Raymond Chandler -- inside a stuffed Great Egret that was in my guest house. It belonged to Spencer Baird. Annie used the pictures to get the down payment on her house in Tucson. She said she figured I would need them one day."

"Did your father ask for the proof?"

"No, he knew right away what I was talking about. He knew Annie and I were allies."

"I love that you wrote a number down on a piece of paper," I said. "Like in the movies."

"I did rather enjoy it."

"I keep thinking of your mother," I said. "Helping your father during his illness after the way he treated her for years."

"No need to pity my mother. She's been living a quite fulfilled life. She saw Europe with friends, she spent time with Annie and her two girls, often visited my other sister, Cassie in San Francisco."

Lily smiled. "You see, mother got her own copies of Annie's photographs."

I asked Lily what happened in Taos. She said, It was paradise for four years. After Jaymes's marriage got annulled, they rented a condo with an indoor clay fireplace. Jaymes worked as a massage therapist at a spa and led yoga classes. Lily painted and worked at the Harwood Museum of Art.

"Perfect, right?" Lily said. "And then I went and destroyed our wonderful life."

Lily and Jaymes had an argument. "Petty to me – I got paint on the refrigerator door again," Lily said. "With Jaymes nothing is petty, it's all about principal."

Lily went to a bar with a friend. A man she had seen at a few poetry readings, stopped to say hello and he and Lily chatted. When Lily's friend left, the man took a seat.

"He was gorgeous," Lily said. "The kind of eyes you want to fall into. His name was Brent Rock. I'm serious; he showed me his driver's license. He hiked and fly fished and wrote poetry. I had one too many Mango Margaritas and went home with him. You know, to show me some of his poems. He opened some wine, we ended up in bed. I know, Eleanor. It went against everything I stood for. But I was curious. And drunk. And very stupid.

"Well, I woke up – more like came to – and felt this terror. Paralyzing guilt and shame. When I got home I broke down crying and told Jaymes. She was devastated. I can't believe I said this, but I said 'It didn't mean anything.' Jaymes told me to move out."

"Then came the intermission," I said.

"Yes. The intermission. I drove back to Woods Hole shattered. I told mother things didn't work out and spent most of my waking hours painting. Imagine father's reaction if he knew?

"Three years later I got a four-page letter from Jaymes. She had forgiven me. Jaymes said she weighed a life together against the weight of one night and realized she would spend the rest of her days regretting our parting. She wanted me to pay a cost— which I certainly did – and realized she was also paying it. The bottom line was she loved me. That much time apart taught her that.

"I wrote back saying I was still single, of course I still loved her and would she like to come here? The next week she moved in with me. It's been heaven since. She has her yoga classes and I have my painting and I am so fortunate to be able to say we still have each other."

DANCING NAKED

Lily said Jaymes did not come to the café because "she has her meditation time at home and I have my time here. Evenings, we have our time together."

It was five days before Christmas. I got to the cafer later than usual because I was shopping on line. There was a Christmas tree near the door in front of the bookcase and beside Mason, who was in a cushy, well-worn chair reading. The Beach Boys were singing "Little Saint Nick."

The three women who walked five miles every dawn before ending up here, were singing. So was Naomi.

Well, way up north where the air gets cold
There's a tale about Christmas that you've all been told
And a real famous cat all dressed up in red
And he spends the whole year workin' out on his sled...

The Elvis question on the white board was a tough one.

Understandably, Naomi said she did not expect to give out a free coffee and scone today.

Lenny's question obviously was for me.

Elvis Presley cut his first acetate at Sun Studios in Memphis for $3.98. What were the two songs on it?

I looked over at Lily and she waved. I exaggerated a shrug and a look of dread and shook my head.

"Are you fucking kidding me?" the man behind me bellowed. I turned. He was wearing a Santa outfit without the beard and a Red Sox cap. His breath smelled of Christmas cheer for breakfast.

"Watch your language." It was Big Mack. An ex-cop and now security guard at the Oceanographic Institute , Big Mack looks like he can lift two Santas over his head.

"HOUND DOG," the man barked.

"Wait your turn, Santa," Naomi said.

"DON'T BE CRUEL."

Naomi glared at him.

"JEEZUS. You gotta come up with another question."

"Against the rules," Naomi said. The customer in front of me took her coffee and scone, caught my eye, shook her head and smiled.

"How can there be rules," Santa said. "It's a friggin trivia game."

Lenny and May appeared at the counter. "It's not trivia," Lenny said. "And there are rules because it's my music quiz."

"Have a cup on the house," May said. "Merry Christmas."

Santa ignored her.

Lenny grabbed a card from a pile on the counter on which his rules were written, held it out, said, "Here."

Santa took it, ripped it up and let the pieces fall.

"Alright, you're out of here," Lenny said and walked around the counter.

"You can't throw me out."

"I bet I can," Lenny said as Big Mack and two other men surrounded Santa. Heads were turned. Chuck Berry was singing "Run, Run Rudolph."

"Your music quiz sucks," Santa said, turned and walked out, tilting slightly.

I exhaled and tried to remember the two Elvis songs; I knew I had read about that first acetate. I even knew Sun Studio was on Union Avenue in Memphis.

"Well?" said Naomi.

"Was one of the songs, 'That's Alright Mama?'" My stomach was tight.

Naomi made a TV-game-show-wrong-answer-buzzer sound. I paid for my coffee and scone and took them to our table. Why did I feel like my math teacher Mr. Colby just flunked me?

"What were they? The two songs?" Lily asked.

"No idea."

"Come on. You're playing possum."

"I wish."

"Boy, will Lenny be gloating," Lily said.

On cue, I heard Lenny say loudly, "The Elvis lady goes down."

Lily looked past me toward the counter. I turned. Santa was back in line.

"It's that guy from before," I said.

"I'll go alert Lenny," Lily said and got up and went behind the counter. "Like a good deputy."

Lenny's most important rules: No answering the quiz if you connect to the internet before getting in line and after leaving the line. That guarded against someone reading the question, and then going to a table or outside to research the answer on a phone or laptop.

"This is a quiz based on knowledge and memory," Lenny would bark. "Not Google and Bing."

Eyes were needed to spy cheaters. Lenny deputized his regulars, a.k.a., his family.

"Free week of coffees for anyone nabbing a researcher," Lenny told us.

Every so often, Skip or Dr. Jane or Lily saw a newcomer on the Internet before going to the counter and they informed Lenny. Someone actually saw a man with binoculars outside reading the question. Of course, this system was far from foolproof. But no one said that to Lenny.

Santa got to the counter swaying slightly.

"I wanna answer the question," he said loudly. "I know the two songs." Before Naomi could say anything, he coughed up, "Your Happiness," and, "That's When Your Heartache Begins."

"Um, that's right," Naomi said. "But this is your second time in line, so--"

"Screw that. Give me my free coffee."

"This is where your heartache begins," Lenny told Santa, having heard the commotion. "You went and looked it up, right?"

"Yeah. So?"

"So, you're not allowed. Maybe if you'd read the rules." Lenny pounded a finger down on the pile of rule cards.

"Fuck the rules. No one knows shit about Elvis without looking it up."

"Not today, apparently," Lenny said loudly, craning his neck to look over at me.

"Now I know the answer," Santa said. "I want my free coffee."

When he said, "coffee,' he threw his hands out and his left one knocked a large black coffee out of Buck's hand.

"We've had about enough of you," Mack said as he put a hand on each side of Santa, lifted him and pointed him toward the door.

When Mack put him down, Santa stumbled to his left, grabbed the Christmas tree and pulled it with him to the floor.

That's when Mack grabbed Santa by the wide belt, slid him from beneath the still-lit tree, lifted him and forced him out the door. "I want my free coffee," could be heard through the window.

There was laughter while the tree was up-righted. David came with a dust pan and broom for the needles. Customers picked up the dozen ornaments. "Told you, May. Plastic ornaments are best," came Lenny's voice.

Just then there was a crash through a window pane above the political junkies, sprinkling shards on their table. Santa had grabbed the "Open" sign out front and crashed it through the glass.

"An Obama supporter," John said. "What's that have to do with Obama?" Ed said, and Lenny and Big Mack ran out and I saw Mack bear-hug Santa and Lenny grab the pole and heard the man yell about free coffee.

When the police drove off with Santa, Tom Petty was singing, "Don't come around here no more," as were most everyone in the café, thanks to Naomi.

The first time I ever found myself inside the Byrds' Song Café was a lonely Thanksgiving morning. Harris had promised his parents we would spent the holiday with them in Mystic, Connecticut.

Harris waited until Tuesday of Thanksgiving week to tell me.

"I told you weeks ago I couldn't go," I said, pounding a pillow. "I have to work, remember? I have fall cleanups to do. Oceans of leaves, Harris. Which isn't really the point. The point is, we talked about it. We decided. And you go ahead and plan it anyway."

Harris does not argue, which infuriates me. He stands there with his head tilted and a sad expression like I am the one hurting his feelings.

"Remember when you brought it up three weeks ago we agreed to have Thanksgiving here together because I had to work?"

"I thought that was tentative," he said.

"No. We agreed. When did you talk to your parents?"

"Last week."

"Why didn't you check with me then?"

"I knew you'd say no."

"Oh, and I'd say yes at the last minute?"

"Fine. OK. I'll call my parents and tell them you don't want to spend Thanksgiving with them."

"You're not going to put this on me, Harris."

"Why can't you finish your cleanups in December?"

"That's not the point." I took a lengthy breath. "How long did you tell them we'd stay."

"Through the weekend."

"You didn't think about my work. Only yourself. As usual."

"Sorry."

I finished making the bed while Harris stood there as if my mind would change if he merely waited.

"So," he said. "You're not going."

"NO. I...AM...WORKING."

"But, baby, they're expecting us."

I TOLD YOU BEFORE. DON'T CALL ME BABY.

"Yeah, I know, that's reserved for your husband. I thought you'd be over that."

"I don't want to be over it. Look, Harris. You go to your parents. Tell them what you want. I had to work, I didn't want to go, whatever."

"You don't mind?"

"I'd rather you went."

"OK then."

I put an Elvis record on my turntable, put on my headphones and sat in the recliner. I laughed and shook my head at the pathos. The loving companion was supposed to apologize for ignoring my needs. He was supposed to stand up to his parents, assure me we will have a nice, quiet Thanksgiving together. He is supposed to offer to cook and even help me with the leaves. Harris is supposed to think about me instead of himself. He is certainly not supposed to go ahead and leave me alone because he is afraid what his parents might think. But this is Harris. I did feel sympathy and sadness because he is not intentionally mean, only incapable of thinking of my feelings.

His selfishness took root with the little things. The day we were at the mall and there was an Orange Julius stand. My father used to buy his high school sweetheart an Orange Julius on their dates and she turned out to be my mother. My brother shared an Orange Julius with his girlfriend, whom he ended up marrying. "We have to try it," I told Harris. On the way home I told Harris my sentimental Orange Julius story.

The next day Harris comes home drinking an Orange Julius. "Man, these are good," he said.

"You only got one for yourself?" I asked.

"Why?" Harris said. "Did you want one?"

When Harris said he was going to bring home a poinsettia at Christmastime, I told him to please don't because our cat would get sick if she chewed on it -- she likes to chew all our plants – but he brought one home anyway.

It seemed every time I went to the refrigerator for cream, the carton contained a few drops. If I sat reading with the TV on, he'd change the channel, then say, "You weren't watching that, were you?" Of course, he never put down the toilet seat. And right after sex, he would jump up and go put on the ballgame.

When I moved from my apartment to his house, I told myself it is just Harris adjusting or he has not shaken behavior he learned from his father (which was true, I later learned, watching Harris's mother wait on her husband one entire weekend).

The past summer I spent much of my day, while I planted and pruned and weeded, asking myself why I did not split up with Harris. Fear of being alone? The times when he was affectionate, fun and would actually wash laundry and houseclean without being hounded? Was it his nice house, equidistance from downtown and the ocean, with a sizable shed for my tools? Because he does not drink a lot, or do drugs, and is basically a good guy? Was I waiting for a return to that romantic time when we met?

Two years ago on a clear fall morning, I was gassing up my red Ford Ranger, when I noticed a dark-haired man on the other side of the pump. He caught my eye and smiled. I smiled back. "Taking on any more work?" he asked.

"I might," I said. He asked how long I landscaped, what I specialized in, and what he wanted done on his property. My gas tank overflowed, and he apologized for distracting me, which I thought was more polite than laughing. I pointed to the side of my truck, where it said, "Eleanor's Mini-Scape" with my phone number. "Give me a call if you want me to take a look," I said.

The next day he left a voice mail. His name was Harris and could I give him an estimate for cleaning up his property?

My regular clients were my priorities, but there was time for him the following week. I returned the call, got his address and went at noon the next day, a Saturday. He showed me around his small Cape-style house. He wanted a forsythia pruned here, a pruned Rose of Sharon there, and two tarps worth of leaves removed. Harris obviously was fit. Why not do it himself?

I thought either he a) was very lazy; b) totally inept at doing even minor yard work or c) just wanted to get me to his place.

"You know, I called because it was a sure way to see you again," he said, blushing. He brought me coffee, and asked me about myself, and appeared interested. He was concerned about attracting dangerous men, because my phone number was on my truck. I had spent the past few years, when I finally felt I could date, wasting time on Internet dating sites. I met men who lied about their looks, or spent hours talking about their jobs, their cars, and how much they worked out. Meeting Harris was serendipitous. He was also very attractive, and said he played guitar.

I gave Harris an estimate for the work. We shook hands. "Hey," he said when I turned toward my truck, "I'm headed over to Rita's Diner for a sandwich. You want to join me? Follow me over?"

"Sure," I said. "But separate checks, OK?"

"Don't worry, it's not a date. Just two people having lunch."

Harris owned an eyeglass shop on Main Street. I got a kick out of the fact he wore glasses with non-prescription glass in public to display the latest styles.

"Free advertising," he said. "Sort of like a car dealer driving next year's model around town ."

Our first official date was the day after I finished work in his yard. We had a picnic overlooking Nobska Point, took a long walk and went to the artsy cinema to see Crazy Heart – my choice. He gave me white roses, "for new beginnings." On our third date Harris gave me a CD. "Made this for you. Tell me if you like it," he said.

The next morning, on the way to one of my clients, the Finnegans, to weed their gardens and edge the beds, I inserted the CD. No one since Mitch had ever similarly wooed me.

Harris was strumming guitar and singing. The song was Elenore by The Turtles from '68. My brother had the 45 and used to tease me by singing it when I was 14.

You got a thing about you
I just can't live without you
I really want you, Elenore, near me
Your looks intoxicate me
Even though your folks hate me
There's no one like you, Elenore, really

Elenore, gee I think you're swell
And you really do me well
You're my pride and joy, et cetera…

I remembered the different spelling of Eleanor but it did not matter. I laughed, I was delighted. I looked forward to seeing him.

At Christmas, six weeks after we met, he told me he loved me while we made love. Afterward, lying beside him, I said, "Are you sure?"

"About what?"

"You said you love me."

"Of course."

"It's OK if you didn't mean it. I understand you say things while you're intimate."

"No. I am sure. But I guess it was too soon for you."

"No. I think I love you, too."

"You think?"

"I do. I love you, Harris."

But I was not sure. I was sure with Mitch. With Harris, I felt a void filled. Companionship. I settled for that, figuring over-the-cliff love would come later. I was still waiting, two years later.

A few month ago, when I got tired of asking myself why I stay with Harris, I went to a counselor to ask her.

Lisa Wu listened and nodded. "Maternalism," she finally said during our third session.

"Harris and I are 40. I don't want to be his mother," I said. "Come up with something else."

Three more sessions of frustration on both our parts followed. Finally, Lisa said, "Look. What you are going through is normal. The closer you grow to someone, the more of their flaws and defects you see. If you love that person, the defects are tolerable, like cleaning up after your dog. Even charming. Ergo, you might not love Harris. Spend some time apart and see how your heart feels."

On that, we agreed.

The five days Harris spent with his parents at Thanksgiving provided that separation.

I was still in bed when Harris left to go to Connecticut. He bent to kiss me and said he would call. "Don't work too hard," he said.

It was good alone. No tiptoeing around while Harris slept. I could play some Elvis while I dressed and had breakfast and did not have to hear Harris's obnoxious Elvis impersonation. I had promised my favorite client, Dr. Solomon, to get his leaves up before Thanksgiving, so I went to his house. When I checked my cell at noon, there was a message from Harris. His parents and brothers are all sorry I could not make the trip, he said.

"Yes, but are you sorry, Harris," I said to no one, and flipping the phone onto the passenger seat, went back to my leaf blower, looking forward to being alone that night.

Thanksgiving morning I called my parents in Florida. Then I spoke to Harris, then his mother. I realized part of me missed him. I wished that part didn't. I can't live with or without you.

It was warmish, in the high 40s, so I walked to the beach road and headed on the sidewalk up along the bluffs overlooking Vineyard Sound.

Not wanting to be inside when I returned home, I went for a drive and ended up in Woods Hole. After driving over the Woods Hole drawbridge I saw an "Open" sign hanging on a pole in front of a storefront. "Byrds' Song Café" it said above the door. I had heard a woman in the supermarket telling a friend about the place. "Don't go if you don't like music while you have your coffee," she said.

I parked. Walking past the front windows, I saw how crowded the place was, heard muffled voices singing and wondered whether it was a private holiday party.

I stepped inside and stopped. People were seated in mismatched wood chairs at a dozen wood tables. In queen Anne chairs by a window, all were singing "Eleanor Rigby" by the Beatles, another song my brother sang to me.

At the far wall, a man sat at an upright piano playing. Beside him, a woman was belting out the song..
Eleanor Rigby died in the church and was buried along with her name
Nobody came
Father McKenzie wiping the dirt from his hands as he walks from the grave
No one was saved
All the lonely people
Where do they all come from?

I walked closer to the woman singing. I could not believe it. She was wearing a '60s Beatle wig. Just like the one my mother told me dad wore when he sang, "All My Loving" to her. A sweet memory.

High above the counter I examined the chalkboard menu: dozens of coffees and teas. "What's going on?" I asked the young woman I later found out was Naomi, as she made my café au lait.

"The woman singing is Doctor Jane. It's her 70th birthday," Naomi said, and pointed to a white board to her right. "If you answer the music quiz question correctly on your birthday, Lenny makes you get up and sing an appropriate song."

On the white board, it said, "Welcome to the Byrds' Song Café." Someone had drawn two chirping birds and notes above them.

Beneath that:

Today's Quiz Question

How did Paul McCartney come up with the name Eleanor Rigby?

"What was the answer?" I asked Naomi.

She picked up a piece of paper and read:

"From actress Eleanor Bron, who had starred with the Beatles in the film Help! And a store in Bristol called Rigby & Evans Ltd, Wine & Spirit Shippers."

"And that woman Dr. Jane knew that?" I said, my voice rising.

"If it's about '60's music, Dr. Jane knows it. Yesterday, there's this Dylan question? What song mentions Galileo's math book, John the Baptist and a fantastic collection of stamps? Right away Dr. Jane announces, 'Tombstone Blues.' She's amazing. And she doesn't look this stuff up. That's against the number one rule. No researching."

"How do you enforce such a rule?"

"Lenny's got his deputies."

"And who's Lenny?"

"He was the one at the piano. He's the owner, and my dad. Someone here can explain it all to you. OK?"

"What is that amazing aroma?"

"Oh, that's my mom's homemade scones. Would you like one?"

"How could anyone refuse? Oh, I'm sorry," I said to a couple waiting behind me because I was holding them up.

"No worries," the man said. "Always good to see a newbie."

Just then, I thought, I feel like I'm home.

Early the next morning I loaded rakes, my backpack blower and two tarps into the Ranger and headed to Woods Hole before going to a client's house. I got to the cafe shortly after it opened. There was some soft Joni Mitchell playing, "A Case of You." James Taylor on guitar, I thought to myself standing at the counter. I read the music question.

Who did Eric Clapton write Layla for and who was she married to at the time?

"Good morning," Naomi smiled. "Welcome back."

"Thank you. I'll try the spicy Mexican mocha latte. And I'll have a scone."

While Naomi went to work I said, "Pattie Boyd and she was married to George Harrison."

"You got yourself free mocha latte and a scone. Congrats," Naomi said. "Thought it would take at least until 7:30 for someone to get that question right."

"Sorry. Should have let others have a chance…"

"No, you deserve it. Enjoy." She placed the drink and plated scone on the counter.

"Well done," came the voice behind me. I turned and was taken aback by this tall gorgeous woman in a blue Southwestern coat.

"It's embarrassing that I actually know the answer," I said.

"Why do you think that?"

"It's useless information."

"Nonsense."

The woman got out of line. "Can I talk to you a minute?" she said. I followed her away from the counter.

"Let me ask you this. What does the song 'Layla' remind you of?" she said.

"Oh, spin the bottle. I was in ninth grade and for some reason, I was friendly with the three most mature girls in school. Diane Beck, Paula Franey and Debbie Neckes. I still remember. They were way ahead of me sexually. They told me Dougie Hart was having a party and I was invited. Actually, they asked me so there'd be four girls and four guys. Dougie had his brother's records out and played the Layla album while we played spin the bottle. I kissed Rodney Manning. Boy, I had a crush on him. I remember it was a sloppy kiss, like a water fountain. Next day at school Dougie said his brother smacked him because Layla got scratched."

"See?" the woman said. "It's not useless information. It's music. It's your life."

I thanked her and she asked me to sit with her.

"I'm Lily," she said and held out her hand. "Isn't this a wonderful place."

"Music, coffee, singing, camaraderie. It's idyllic," I said.

Lily removed her coat to reveal a red western shirt. She said it belonged to a friend she had in New Mexico. Lily admired it and when Andy was dying of AIDS he gave it to her. "Every time I wear this shirt I think about Andy when it fit him," she said.

We both started on our scones by forking some whipped cream. "Another thing about music being important," said Lily after wiping her lips with a napkin. "I once asked the man who owns this café, Lenny, why he chose to incorporate music. He said because music is not like people. Music never lets you down and doesn't lie. You can depend on music."

That's why I always stuck with Elvis, I said to myself.

Something stirred and settled inside me while we talked. I felt free of worry, loneliness and a Harris conundrum. It was like a date that was going well; couldn't the men I met between Mitch and Harris have been like Lily? Then, there was this thought: I don't need a man right now if I have this.

Lily asked me about my job, interests and love life. I told her all about Harris the following morning.

"Two years, huh?" Lily said. "And Harris has not filled your needs."

"Well, some."

"I've only known you, what, three hours? But it sounds like he does not meet your important needs. He's company, he provides a home, things like that. But sacrificing for you, having compassion, thinking of your feelings -- doesn't sound like it."

"I talked to a shrink," I said. "She said all his flaws that still bother me a lot? Love would make dealing with them worth it. So I must not love him."

"Eleanor. Love is not something to ponder. You know if you love him. Love is not contingent on your partner being perfect. If it isn't there, you need to decide if you want to keep searching for true love, or live with Harris because it's better than nothing. And there's sex, and usually, life's pretty good. One thing's for sure. Harris will not walk in one day and make your heart soar."

"What you're saying is it's not going to get better."

"There's a woman, Sarah, who comes here. She's a poet. She started writing when she was 13. Well, she kept at it through high school and college, got her MFA, and finally had her first chapbook published. She got a box of them in the mail, opened it and held a copy in her hand. She said she felt no different. She felt depressed for a week."

"Why?" I asked.

"She said she knew right then she had the wrong idea about being published. When she'd work on a poem for quite a while and finish it, she'd feel satisfaction. Then, when she read it at a workshop or a reading and people told her it was good, she'd feel a high like no other. It didn't get any better than that."

"So, I have the wrong idea about a relationship. It doesn't get any better than the courting."

"Good girl."

"Lily, I wasted good money on a shrink."

To Lily's credit, she did not once criticize me for plodding on with Harris once he was back from Connecticut. I told her Harris apologized for leaving me alone and asked me if I wanted to spend Christmas with my parents. I told him staying home relaxing sounded better. "Sounds like some progress," Lily said. "Maybe the time apart helped."

But what about love? You think that will just appear under the tree? I did not tell Lily I was reading her mind.

Lily and Jaymes flew to Arizona Dec. 21 to be with Lily's sister and nieces for Christmas. I spent a few days helping the James, the owner of the town's busiest florist, with arrangements, which I do occasionally in winter. Mostly the flowers are for wakes.

Lily said she would see me at the café the day after Christmas.

"What's got into you?" she said when she sat. "I saw your big smile from outside."

"Naomi," I called out. She had her signal. She played "Graceland" by Paul Simon.

I was still smiling and bobbed to the music. The Mississippi Delta was shining like a national guitar…

"Tell me you're going to Graceland," Lily said, her brown eyes wide.

Paul Simon and I sang. I'm going to Graceland, Graceland in Memphis, Tennessee…

Yes, I told Lily, My dream of going to Elvis's home, to Memphis, was coming true.
I opened a large, nearly weightless box Christmas morning, removed layers of tissue and found two airline tickets to Memphis. Harris also made reservations at the Heartbreak Hotel across the street from the Graceland mansion. He could not have given me a better gift.

"We're leaving tomorrow," I said, "and we'll be back the 30th. Graceland closes the next day until March."

"But Harris doesn't like Elvis," Lily said. "You said he ridicules him."

"That's what I said. I asked him if he was sure he wanted to go. Harris said he will enjoy it because I will. He promised to behave. No making fun of Elvis, no impersonations, just enjoying the tours."

Lily told me to be cautious. And she told me a story about a couple she knew in Taos.

Charles's wife, Tia, was nuts about Melissa Etheridge. Charles could not stand to listen to her, made fun of her lyrics because he considered them shallow.

"Well, on Tia's birthday, Charley presents her with two tickets to see Melissa Etheridge," Lily said. "I'll take Lily. she says. Charley says, "They're for us.

She laughs.

He says he'd dead serious. He wants to experience her joy, yadda yadda.

They go. Etheridge starts singing, 'My Lover.'

My lover makes me weak, gives me breath to speak
My lover takes me home, cools the rolling stone
my lover's thorny kiss, the reason to exist.

Charley yells out sarcastically, "Oh, that's deep, and keeps telling Tia about how Etheridge can't write, can't sing, and sounds like screeching tires.

Tia walks out, before the concert's over. They get in the car and Tia's in tears. Charley, he's pissed because she left. Imagine? He's the asshole and he's pissed."

"They still together?"

"God, no."

I imagined Harris doing something similar. I shook the thought away.

Harris and I stood at 706 Union Ave., Memphis. Sun Studios, the world's most famous record studio. "That's it?" Harris said.

"What did you expect?" I said. "The size of a WalMart."

"No, just more impressive."

"Look, Harris, if you don't want to come in..."

"Of course I do."

We walked inside, to join the tour group, to where Jerry Lee Lewis and Johnny Cash and Carl Perkins recorded. This is it. This is where 18-year-old Elvis stood fidgety, mumbling about recording an acetate disk. This is where he came later to record 'That's Alright' with a band in front of the great Sam Phillips. This is where history began. Where I am standing.

"Well-a bless-a my soul-a what's wrong with me…" Harris mimicked Elvis on "All Shook Up." Horribly, as usual.

The people on the tour shook their heads and scowled as one. Hopefully making a point, I had told Harris it would be like imitating Pope Benedict at St. Peter's.

"Harris, stop it," I said.

"Oh, lighten up."

I said nothing more, just listened to the tour guide.

Afterward, I told Harris I would go to Graceland alone. I was saving Elvis's mansion for our last day in Memphis so it would be my freshest memory on the flight home.

"Come on, I'm sorry," Harris said. "It was stupid. Tomorrow, at Graceland I'll be quiet and if I get bored, I'll just wait outside. No big deal."

At least he didn't call me baby, I thought.

We had a rented a car and went to see places from Elvis's youth; the Rainbow Rollerdome, where he kissed his first girlfriend; Charlie's Record Shop, where he got a NuGrape at the soda fountain and a juke box always played. There was a knot in my stomach the entire time. Harris next wanted to go to Beale Street. I told him to drop me at the hotel, take the car, and go where he wanted.

In the hotel lobby, I sat and called my mother. It felt good to talk to her and hear how happy she was for me. Then, I decided to go walking to find my mother the souvenir she wanted: an Elvis doll that talks and sings in his voice.

I walked past the front desk and saw a man handing a hotel key to the clerk. He looked familiar. I moved closer.

"Cory?"

He turned. "Eleanor? Oh, my God."

Cory Beck was the clarinet player in Mitch's Dixieland band. We talked a few times and the last time was at Mitch's funeral. His curly black hair was shorter, he still was in shape and had a great smile.

We hugged. "Oh, what a drag. I'm just checking out," he said.

I told him I lived in Falmouth and still landscaped. Cory lived in Cotuit, worked for a home improvement company. He was officially divorced two weeks ago.

"I dealt with it by taking time off from work and traveling a bit," he said. "I went to Florida to do some fishing. Then, I figured, what the hell. I always wanted to get to Graceland. Now, I'm flying to Cleveland to see the Rock & Roll Hall of Fame. Then, home."

"Mitch never told me you were into Elvis," I said.

"Oh, yeah. Love the King. So, who are you here with?"

"A friend. He's out sightseeing."

"Man, it's great to see you."

Cory said he wished we could meet up for dinner but he had to get to the airport. I walked out with him. "Let me give you my number," he said. "Call when you get back and we'll catch up." He took a business card from his wallet and wrote the cell number on the back. Then, I watched him place a suitcase inside an airline shuttle van and get inside.

The knot in my stomach was gone. In its place was a desire to get to know Cory.

The next morning I decided nothing would ruin the tour of Graceland Mansion. While I was dressing, Harris took two rum nips from the mini-bar and mixed himself a rum and Coke.

"Need some help to get through this, do you?" I said.

"Hey, we're on vacation," he said. When he finished his drink, Harris poured another nip into the Coke can and took it with him. "One for the road," he said.

Harris gulped down the drink outside, tossed the can in a trash receptacle and we walked across the road to the mansion. In front of the mansion, I handed a woman from Iowa my camera and posed for a photograph. We stepped inside. I was mesmerized.

There was the 15-foot white sofa in the foyer. "Is this where he ate his friend banana sandwiches?" Harris said. I ignored him. We got to the Jungle Room and there was the floor-to-ceiling shag carpet. "Hunka hunka burning love," Harris kept singing.

And then we were in the Racquetball Trophy Room, where Elvis's costumes are enclosed in glass cases.

"Hey, where's the bathroom where he died with his pants down around his ankles," Harris called out.

I walked out of Graceland Mansion just as a security guard got to Harris.

While we were in the air, I decided to break up with Harris. I did not tell him because who wants to listen to a couple arguing on a plane?

I was looking out the window at what I guessed was Kentucky on Flight 211 – my brother's birthday; so much for good omens – when it came to me. I realized I had been telling myself to stay with Harris because I am 40 and at least I have someone. Aren't you supposed to when you're 40? Bullshit.. I don't have to stay with Harris. Eleanor, you just let yourself off the hook. You are free.

"Yes," I exclaimed and raised a fist.

"What?" Harris said.

"Nothing."

Harris returned to sipping his beer. He exhaled. He said it seemed I did not have a great time in Memphis and after he spent so much money on a trip, I should have been happier.

"You asshole." I stood up. "Excuse me. Would anyone like a window seat? I'll gladly switch with you. I get a little queasy when I look out and I wouldn't want the view to go to waste."

Harris was saying, "What is wrong with you? What did I say?" while I nudged my way past him. A strong-perfumed, rouge-cheeked gray haired woman had stood up. She was wearing an Elvis pin. "Well, if there are no other takers…" she said and she got in beside Harris, who was trying to get a flight attendant's attention.

Sitting in an aisle seat a few rows behind Harris, I must have felt some relief because I fell asleep. I dreamed of being kissed passionately and awoke with the realization it was Lily. My next thought did not leave me. I wanted the dream to be real.

Harris must have done some thinking on the plane because when we were on the bus at Logan Airport bound for Woods Hole, he said, "I'm sorry, Eleanor."

"Sorry for what?"

"Doing my stupid impersonations."

"Remember before we left, you assured me? You said you wouldn't…Oh, forget it. It doesn't matter."

I wanted to say, I just don't feel anything, Harris, I'm done, I'm gone. No, Lily wait until we get home; this is not the place.

Harris slept on the bus. I thought of something Lily said. "Remember how you said the only music Harris owns are Greatest Hits CDs? Maybe that says something about willingness to commit emotionally."

I wanted it to be morning with Lily.

At Woods Hole we took another bus to Falmouth and a cab to Harris's house. It was nearly midnight. I told Harris I was moving out as soon as I found an apartment. I blamed myself for us splitting up. His reaction was to pout, go to the bedroom, not even slam the door. He doesn't have any fight in him, I thought to myself.

On the sofa in the dark I was aroused by thoughts of Lily. It's normal, she's beautiful, I told myself. Don't all women in a sex rut fantasize about women?

At the café I placed a gift on the table and sat to wait for Lily. "For you," I said to Lily when she sat. "For you, Eleanor," Naomi called out. The song "Suspicious Minds" played.

We're caught in a trap

I can't walk out…

"You brought me something" Lily said. "It's sweet."

"Souvenir from Graceland."

Lily unwrapped the present. We both laughed. It was an Elvis Presley Viva Las Vegas simulated leather messenger bag.

"I love it," Lily said. "Tell me, tell me. How was the trip?"

When I finished the details, right up to my decision to move out, Lily did not say, "I told you so." She said she would help me.

She went to the table where Skip was sitting and spoke to him. He nodded and smiled.

Lily returned with Skip behind her. "It's all set," Lily said. "What is?"

Skip told me he would be happy to let me stay in the spare room in his house as long as I needed to. "I insist," he said. "A friend of Lily's is a friend of mine."

On Valentine's Day inside the café I thought about the ones I spent with Mitch, how he always cooked me dinner and made gifts. One year he made a huge collage of photos of us together. Harris just gave me the obligatory roses.

When I was seated with my coffee and scone, Lenny walked over and placed an envelope on the table. "Guy named Harris left this for you," he said. "It ain't ticking."

My first thought was to get up and toss it in the trash basket; I did not want to risk getting lured in by a sappy Valentine's Day card from the man I wanted to be free of. But I opened the envelope. There was a CD and a card. Inside, it read:

Dear Eleanor,

I am sorry we split up. Hope you are well.

Love, Harris.

p.s.

How is my heart doing?

"What are you going to do?" Lily said when I showed her the card. She was more radiant than usual in a burgundy colored western shirt.

"Well. I'll listen to the CD and go from there," I said.

The next morning brought four inches of snow. While I shoveled my driveway, I decided to give Harris another chance.

Maybe he was willing to change. At least we could sit and talk about our differences and what I expect out of the relationship. I had to admit my living alone was losing its appeal.

There was another reason for wanting to try again with Harris. I wanted to be attracted to a man again, wanted to make love to a man. I needed reaffirmation. Only that could eradicate this attraction to Lily.

Lily was already at the café using her laptop when I stepped inside the door and pounded my heavy boots on the floor. There were only four others in the café because of the storm.

"You made it," Naomi said from behind the counter.

"Obviously, I'm addicted;" I said and ordered a café au lait and scone. I thought to myself, I'm addicted to Lily as much as I am to the coffee.

"Lily already answered today's question correctly," Naomi said.

"I figured that."

On the whiteboard was this question:

According to legend, what musician mastered the guitar after having it tuned by the devil at a Mississippi crossroad?

Robert Johnson, Lily told me when I sat. "Glad you have your laptop," I said. "Listen to this." I handed her the CD. "Harris has a home recording studio, some digital to analog converter or something."

Lily took headphones from her bag, connected them to the computer and put them on. She slid the CD into the hard drive. I smiled and sipped while she listened.

"Clever," she said when she finished listening.

Harris had recorded the song "Eleanor" by Low Millions. He sang and played guitar – not well, but that was not the point.

"He actually found this song that says 'I won't call you baby anymore,'" I said. "Isn't that sweet?"

"Like I said, it's clever," Lily said. "But doing something special for you on Valentine's Day doesn't erase how you've felt about him for a long time. All you've done is fall in love with this grand gesture. Romance is easy from a distance. You want a perfect relationship? Trade greeting cards and CDs but don't ever get together. Just stay infatuated."

"He could be different, now, Lily," I said, putting the CD in my jacket pocket.

Lily looked at me, smiled and shook her head. "Didn't you hear the line in the song, 'you go your way and I'll go mine?' Doesn't sound very romantic."

I never did call Harris. And he didn't call me, baby, anymore.

On a Saturday in April, I agreed to let Lily paint my portrait.

In Skip's extra bathroom I spent an hour on my makeup. I spread out four blouses on the bed. I held up the lavender one and looked in the mirror. Lily told me to wear something understated. I went back to the closet and took out my white blouse. It had a wraparound front, buttoned, long sleeves and a deep v-neck. I knew what I was doing. I wanted to look sexy.

With the blouse on I could hear my heartbeat. I craved. I craved what I had none of and could not decide how to fulfill the craving. I left for the gallery.

I had been in Lily's gallery six times to bring her coffee or her favorite turkey club sandwich from Bernadine's. Each time I could not believe the realism of her portraits. I was surprised to see one of Raven on the wall.

DANCING NAKED

Raven came to the café mornings for coffee to go. She had hair the color of a red lava lamp and was always braless and wore t-shirts with sayings like NO ONE KNOWS I'M A LESBIAN. One morning she wore yoga pants, a black t-shirt emblazoned with "ASK, TELL." She stopped at our the table and said to Lily, "You look soooo great today," then something I couldn't hear into Lily's ear.

Lily stood up. Raven came up to Lily's breast.

"Why don't you take whatever incarnation of butchness you re presenting this week and shoo," said Lily, waving a hand.

"Screw, bitch," Raven said and left the café.

"Hard to believe we were once friends," Lily said.

"Eleanor?" came Lily's voice from her studio when I was inside the gallery. "Would you mind locking the door and hanging up the 'Closed' sign? I'll be just a minute."

Lily wore a tapered white western shirt with purple embroidery on the shoulders and jeans that wore swatches of paint. She gave me a hug. "You look fantastic. Except for the makeup," Lily said. "Remember what I said? I want to capture your natural beauty. The way you look on a work day. I love that. Please wash it off."

I scrubbed my face in the tiny restroom in Lily's studio, which was a separate room from the gallery. There were paintings leaning against a wall, paints on shelves, and a canvas on an easel. There also was a refrigerator and a cot.

I looked at myself in the mirror, feeling good about how I looked without makeup for the first time. I could hear violins, then Tom Waits singing.

DANCING NAKED

Wasted and wounded
It ain't what the moon did
I got what I paid for now...

When I came out, Lily was preparing her paints. "We'll work here because the light is better than in the studio," she said. "Help yourself to some tea. It's herbal. Lemon balm. I don't want you drinking more coffee and having a hard time sitting still. Do you mind the music?"

"Not at all. Which Tom Waits song is that?"

"Tom Traubert's Blues. It's the song that got me into him. Aside from the powerful lyrics, I love how he wove Waltzing Matilda into the song. When I first heard it I called the radio station until someone picked up and could tell me who was singing."

"Who's Tom Traubert?"

"Waits said it was a friend of a friend who died in prison."

She placed a stool beside a window. "It's time to light my subject," she said. I sat and breathed deeply.

Lily squeezed out lines from paint tubes at her palette's edge. She stared at me. From what she told me at one of our coffees about portraits, she was studying me, visualizing colors she needed. Was she seeing warm tones or cool ones and what color is prominent?

"How long will this take?" I asked Lily.

"How long today or how long until the painting is finished?"

"Both."

"I thought we'd do a few hours today, if that's alright. It will take a couple of months to finish."

She took off her shirt to reveal a lace bra. She put the shirt on a hook and took a red plaid flannel shirt down and put that on.

While Lily worked I thought about my job. My landscaping business was going well; all of my clients wanted me for another season and it felt good to know money would be coming in for the next seven months.

It also felt good to be freed from a loveless relationship with Harris. I had time to decide whether I wanted another relationship and time for me.

Something else felt good: Lily's eyes on me.

After two hours I told Lily I needed to use the restroom. "Good time for a break," she said and put her brush down. I stood, stretched and went into the small restroom.

When I opened the bathroom door, Lily was standing there.

She stepped toward me, took both my arms, leaned in and kissed my neck, looked into my eyes, spoke my name and kissed my mouth. I welcomed her tongue and she began to unbutton my blouse while I put my hands through her hair.

Then, after I removed my blouse, Lily released me from my bra and led me to the cot. "Lie down," she said and shed her shirt and bra.

And then I could feel her tongue.

Until there was a loud knock on the door. "Oh, God," said Lily. We reached for our bras. We dressed quickly. There was another knock.

I checked myself in the bathroom mirror while Lily went to the door. I heard Lily say, "I'm sorry; I was in the bathroom. This is such a nice surprise."

"I have a few minutes before my yoga class," came the voice I assumed was Jaymes's. "How is the portrait going?"

"Very well. We were just taking a break."

I was glad I had wiped off my lipstick; surely some would have been on Lily's blouse or neck.

"Eleanor," Lily said. "Come meet Jaymes."

She was more beautiful than I imagined. She had long black hair and was slight like a ballet dancer. I disliked her right away only because she was the one who owned Lily's heart.

"Jaymes, this is Eleanor," Lily said. "She's the portrait I was telling you about this morning. Eleanor is giving it to her mother for her birthday."

I shook Jaymes's hand. She was not smiling. I expected her to say, "I've heard a lot about you." When she didn't, I knew Lily probably never told Jaymes about me. I was glad Lily found it necessary to invent the birthday gift story. That meant I was someone to arouse jealously in Jaymes. I was not just some friend you meet at the coffee shop. I was the threat, the woman you lure to your studio so you can make love to her. My heart raced.

"Why don't we call it a day," Lily said to me.

"Sure," I said. "You want to continue tomorrow? Oh, that's right, it's Sunday; you guys must have plans."

"Maybe tomorrow. We'll talk," Lily said.

When I told Jaymes "it was good to me you," I noticed Lily's baggy shirt was buttoned unevenly. And Jaymes still was not smiling.

When I left the gallery, I wished I had left lipstick on Lily's face. I felt excited. And in my mind's eye, Lily was telling Jaymes she had fallen in love with me, and Jaymes would have to move out.

I walked toward the café, stopped and headed to my truck instead. I decided to buy a bottle of champagne, go home, turn on some music and sit on the deck. I could not remember feeling so giddy.

The next morning brought disappointment and brooding. For just the third time since we met, Lily did not show up at the café.

Monday morning, I got a latte and scone, ignored the quiz question, and sat to wait for Lily. She did not arrive by the time I had to leave to start a spring cleanup at the Lawsons.

First, I stopped at Lily's gallery. It was closed.

Tuesday was Lily's birthday. For weeks I looked forward to her singing at the café. Now, I just hoped to see her.

Before dawn, I drove to Nobska Light with her birthday gift – a western shirt I found on a website -- and was relieved to see Lily's Jeep parked there. I walked across the road, stood on the bluff overlooking Vineyard Sound and saw Lily fishing. The sun began to peer over the horizon to my left.

I walked slowly down a steep rock-laden path to the sea's edge. Lily, wearing waders, stood on a flat boulder of a broken-down jetty. I watched her cast.

"Lily," I called after a few minutes, She turned and looked at me while reeling in her line. I waited for Lily to come speak to me. She didn't.

"Lily," I called again and again she turned. "Can we talk?"

She held her rod with a lure dangling. "Got nothing to say," she said.

"Nothing? How can you say that?"

"OK. I have one thing to say. It was a big mistake."

I shuddered and the tears came. "Goodbye, Lily," I said to the breeze and wept while I strode back up the embankment.

I needed to talk to Lily, needed to tell her the seduction was no mistake. It was what we both wanted.

And wasn't it possible Lily had fallen in love with me?

When I got to the café every seat was filled; surely most were there waiting for Lily. When she walked in, Lenny began singing "Happy Birthday" and everyone, including May, joined in.

That's when I noticed Jaymes seated at a corner table with a man. He leaned toward her, said something and she laughed.

Then Jaymes stood and called out to Lily, waving.

Just a few days before, I felt happier than ever. Now, just standing there, I felt that kicked-in-the-stomach disbelief of losing what you are sure of having.

Lily saw me. I smiled. "Hello, Eleanor," she said.

"Happy Birthday," I said and handed her a gift; I had bought her a western shirt on the Internet.

"Thank you."

"Lily---

"Don't, Eleanor. I'm very fond of you, I really am. But—"

"But it's too late, baby now it's too late though we really did try to make it. This is a Carol King song, right? I'm glad for what we had and how I once loved you. Fine. Go. Your bitch is waiting."

"Love, Eleanor? Come on."

"What, that's not possible?"

"Good bye, Eleanor."

And Lily got behind a woman in line and I waited until she got to the counter to order her coffee and scone and answer the quiz question meant specifically for her:

Tom Waits worked in a pizza place during high school and would later sing about it in two songs. What was its name?

"Napoleone Pizza," Lily said to Naomi, took her coffee and scone and went to sit with Jaymes and their male friend. I stood there not wanting to go outside to the thoughts and loneliness that awaited.

I got a coffee and watched Lenny sit at his piano and begin to play the same opening notes I heard in Lily's gallery. "Tom Traubert's Blues" by Tom Waits.

Lily sang it. She sang strong and hauntingly and no less beautifully than anyone I had heard during my life of loving music.

I looked at Jaymes, who picked up a napkin and wiped a tear. She looked so happy.

And I cried, too, but my tears were those of the forlorn.

When Lily came to the song's finish – and goodnight, Matilda, too – there was applause and whistles and a few bravos.

I rushed out the door and could hear Lenny launching into some Dixieland rag.

Sitting in my truck I stopped shaking and my sadness turned to anger, an anger twisting my insides. How stupid and foolish I had been to give myself to someone who considered me merely a coffee shop friend.

I knew I would never go back to the Byrds' Song Café. Lily would find another to befriend.

I would be a rock and an island because, as the song says, a rock feels no pain and an island never cries.

I drove home. There was all my spring landscape work ahead of me.

DANCING NAKED

DANCING NAKED

ROGUE RADIO

Rocket was on the radio for Dell. That was unusual. That was how they learned about Gail's patrol and Sergeant Gordon. Rocket said he would be out on the late chopper, and would try to bring a hot meal along. When Rocket said things like that, he meant it was a sure thing.

Dell had to tell the guys. The Marys had bonded since taking over Nui Ke. Gail was one of the favorites. And of course, Dell, Cannon and Pete had been with him since Mac brought him out to Mongoose. That seemed a long time ago.

Most of the guys took the news quietly, solemnly, seriously. Water Buffalo exploded in anger. He was screaming mad. Gail was a particular friend for him, and now Water Buffalo was mad. He was mad at the Viet Cong. He was mad at the colonels and generals who made them go out on patrols. He was mad at President Johnson and Secretary of Defense McNamara and the brass who had sent them to Vietnam. He was mad at pretty much everybody. He went out on the perimeter and yelled at the jungle and the mountainside. Everyone let him be. There was no good way to take this news. They liked Sergeant Gordon and they were good… no very good friends with Gail Graham.

Pete was sad for Gail but he had been wounded and knew the routine. He was glad Gail had been treated quickly and would recover from his wounds. Pete thought too about what Nguyen Ba's grandfather had said, and was generally regretful about the war and the price they were all paying. 'And for what?' he wondered.

"You say Redmond's coming out this afternoon. Where's he gonna stay?" asked Pete.

"He can stay with us on Gail's bunk, or he can stay down with the grunts. They have some extra space."

"Yeah, I guess so. I'm just not real excited to see Rocket today. He's the one that assigned us to do these missions and patrols."

"Oh, come on," said Dell. "That's not fair. It doesn't come from him. You're blaming the messenger. Rocket doesn't make those kinds of decisions."

"Yeah. You're right. And I like Rocket. I'm just feeling pretty bad about Gail." Pete blinked back a tear.

"I know. Me too."

The afternoon chopper landed at fifteen thirty. Staff Sergeant Rocket Redmond got off He did bring insulated cans full of hot chow and two five gallon jugs of iced tea. This would last for a while.

Rocket made his way down the rocky pathway to the radio shed. He stuck his head in and called 'hello'. Dell came over from his hootch, and most of the other Marys followed to see what was up.

"Hi. How y'all doin?" Rocket drawled.

"We're sorry to hear about Sergeant Gordon and Gail, and the other guys who took some hits this morning," said Dell.

"Yeah. I'm sure you are. Gail is one of the real good ones. I know y'all been close. We're gonna do everything for him that we can. You know that."

"Is he going to stay at Camp Eagle? Any chance we could stop over to see him when we're in Phu Bai?" asked Cannon.

"Yeah, I think we can work that out. I'll talk with Top about that. I'm sure someone can make a jeep or a three quarter available once in a while for you guys to use, as long as you keep it in Camp Eagle and don't go off base."

"We might need to go to Phu Bai," said Dell.

"Well, we'll work it out. I don't think that will be a problem."

"What do you hear about Mahoney?" Pete asked.

"They tell me he's coming back in a week or so." Rocket said. "He's apparently good as new. They patched up all his holes and fixed his insides, so he's ready to come back with us. How're you doin?"

"Oh, I guess not too bad," Pete laughed. "Just waiting to go home."

"You and every other poor bastard over here. And we're all DEROS-ing at the same time, because we all came together. Hey, that reminds me. I need your R and R destination requests, ASAP. We've got to get you guys started. I think so far only one of you has taken R and R. That was Goldie."

Goldie nodded, "And I can highly recommend Singapore. Nothing but babes." He laughed.

The morning shift was Cat Calhoun, Cannon and Buddha Pierce. They started at oh six thirty, but while they got their breakfast C rations and coffee going, they had the radios on speaker. Buddha was tired of listening to nothing. So were they all. He turned his radio to the Hong Kong BBC news, while they got ready for their shift. The BBC News reporter was telling them about the evening news; young college students had arrived in Chicago to protest the Democratic Party selection for their candidate for President. The Democratic Convention was starting the next day. It was a foregone conclusion at this point that it would be Hubert Humphrey, Vice President, who had only entered the presidential race after President Johnson decided not to run. And then he didn't win any significant primaries against Bobby Kennedy. But, Kennedy was dead and the powers of the party had decided. The young people of America had decided differently, seeing that McCarthy had won some state primaries and Kennedy had won some, and both of them were anti-war candidates. Humphrey was clearly a vote to support the continuation of the Vietnam War and the policies that led to it.

"Now," the BBC announcer said, "the young people were arriving from all over the country to make their voices heard, their anger felt and to embarrass the party leaders who had selected Humphrey in their smoke-filled rooms." They were coming by the hundreds, camping out in the parks along the lakefront. These were the same young people who had protested the war on college campuses, at the White House and the Pentagon, and wherever they could disrupt the flow of military personnel and supplies. They had also worked in the election process going back to New Hampshire primaries and the development of Eugene McCarthy and the anti-war politics. Now, they were being cheated. Their leaders wore their hair long, stringy mustaches and beards and odd clothing and music. Dancing and singing, bra-less and sandaled. Their appearance and their style of politics annoyed the traditionalist leaders, who were affronted by these young activists. Few thought the young people's anti-war politics was serious or well thought out.

"The BBC is talking about our friends, our college student friends," said Buddha. "If I had the chance, I would be there with them."

"You kidding?" replied Cannon. "Those guys are fighting against the war… which is okay, but they're a mess. They have hair down to their ass and look as scraggy as any mountain man ever did… and they're anti-American."

"No, Cannon, they aren't. They are just like you and me, only they don't have to shine their boots every morning and get haircuts. They are willing to go put it on the line for what they believe. They're not sitting home and being polite. They're out there, trying to get something done, just like you are."

"But they have hair down their backs, and they don't wash. They're sleeping with each other whenever they feel like… I just can't get it."

"Cannon. You don't really believe that. Do you?" asked Buddha. "These people are our brothers, our sisters, our cousins, nephews and nieces. These are people who want this war to end, and they are trying to do something about it. They don't believe their government is telling them the truth. And neither do you. We want the war to end, we ought to support these people, anyway we can."

"Yeah, but you can't just take the politics into your own hands and turn things around."

"That's what Humphrey and President Johnson have done," said Buddha. "The young people won the primary elections in state after state, and now the officials of the Democratic Party have taken their victories and turned them around, saying it works for Humphrey."

"But what if these kids make trouble? What if they start riots or protest rallies?" Cannon said.

"Let's wait and see how it plays out. I'll be surprised if this turns into violence. Too many politicians want to be loved by everyone. And the kids aren't trying to make a fight, they want to be heard."

"Shit," said Cannon. "These kids are gonna try something. Wait and see."

Water Buffalo was listening to Armed Forces Radio, AFVN. Pete was listening to BBC from Hong Kong and Monty was listening to BBC from Australia. Nobody was worrying about Vietnamese voice transmissions. They had tried for nearly two months and never found so much as a scratch. So now, they were tuning in to America and what was going on in Chicago. After three days, the

Chicago Police had put on riot gear and tear gas cannons, and tried to bully their way through the young people, to throw them out of the park. Mayor Daley of Chicago was acting like a bully dictator, to the regret of many of the elected politicians who were attending the convention. The young people, to their credit, reacted peacefully and non-violently, which made the police look like fools and brutes.

"We need to do something," said Water Buffalo. "Who knows how to make the radio transmit?"

"We have a standard two way radio. You know, the kind that sits on jeeps or you can carry into the field." Monty said.

"What are you thinking?" asked Pete.

"Have you listened to the Armed Forces Radio version of what's going on? It's bull shit. They won't broadcast the truth to the soldiers in the field because the truth is politically inconvenient. It's too brutish. The cops are acting like Nazi brown shirt thugs. AFVN doesn't want the soldiers to hear the truth."

"They won't play the good music on Armed Forces Radio either," added Cat, "Have you noticed that. The good stuff we can hear in Phu Bai, but we never hear the good music on AFVN. They don't want hard rock or folk music on AFVN."

"Peace music. You mean the Beatles and Cream, the Doors and Janis Joplin?"

"Yeah. A little Jimi Hendrix and throw in some Mothers of Invention too."

"Ooh, man, that would be cool," said Buddha.

"Yeah," said Water Buffalo, "well, what if we broadcast to the soldiers in the field on our grunt radio? What if we were to tell them the truth, and broadcast some cool music?"

"You're nuts. Someone would get in some real trouble, I think." said Sweet Bird. Pete and Monty also joined the conversation.

"No. Not if you don't use your real names. How would they know?"

"You're talking about pissing off some very powerful people. They won't like it."

"If we tell the truth, like we hear it from the BBC, and pass that along to the grunts in the field, what's wrong with that? How much trouble could we get in?"

"Oh, I think we could get in a whole lot of trouble," said Pete. "But Water Buffalo is right. We ought to try to get the truth to the grunts and soldiers in the field. The guys in the base camps too. They all need to hear it."

"And we could have some fun doing it too."

That afternoon, Water Buffalo broadcast his first "Rogue Radio of Vietnam." He talked with Buddha Pierce and Monty Montgomery, everyone used initials so as not to identify themselves.

"Hey," said Water Buffalo. "This is 'Rogue Radio of Vietnam'. We're being brought to you by Jungle Rot and Agent Orange."

"We are going to bring you some of the good music that's going down back stateside, and we're going to tell you some of the news, neither of which you get on Armed Forces Radio. We got tired of waiting for the AFVN boys to get with it, so we're going into competition with them. If you want to hear the straight news, we're gonna tell it to you. If you want to hear the music the folks are humming and listening to at home, we'll play that for you too… "

"So… to start," said Buddha0, "here are the Doors." Buddha had taped a number of the best rock albums onto his reel to reel tapes, which he could broadcast in the shed. He started with 'Break On Through', 'Whiskey Bar' and then 'Light My Fire' and finally

'The End'. While they were playing the music, their frequency was picking up verbal chatter from the grunts. "Keep it up" and "Keep Doing It" were the predominant messages.

After the Doors, Water Buffalo interviewed Buddha and Monty about the protests and fighting in Chicago, and why Buddha wished he could be there, what the young people were fighting for, and for ending the war. After forty minutes of broadcasting, they decided to shut it down. Nobody knew better than they did how radio direction finding could locate a transmitter. When they wrapped it up, they said on the air, "This is Rogue Radio of Vietnam. We'll be back tomorrow. Keep an ear out." As they faded out, they played the Doors' "When the Music's over, turn out the lights, turn out the lights…"

Water Buffalo was ecstatic. He asked the others what they thought, but he never listened to their answers. Pete loved it, but wanted more news and talk. Buddha and Goldie wanted to become disc jockeys, playing lots of mixes of rock music.

Dell was the only wet blanket. "Hey, listen. It was cool," he said. "But I don't think you better keep doing it. You heard some of the responses we got. People out there actually heard it. They were listening. This could get out of control in a hurry."

Maybe because Dell opposed it, Pete decided to champion it. He threw his support to Water Buffalo. "The responses are the reason to keep doing it. This was the first time, and it got through to a bunch of grunts and soldiers. They loved it. They want us to keep it going."

"And what if Captain Burroughs decides to listen in, and gets nosy about it?" asked Dell.

"How is Captain Burroughs or anyone else gonna know that it's us," Pete asked, "unless we shoot off our mouths. Maybe that better be a pledge we take. We have got to keep this to ourselves.

No talking about it when we get to Phu Bai or Camp Eagle."

"I agree with that," Water Buffalo jumped into the conversation. "We all have to swear, no blabbing. Is that right?"

The guys mumbled "yeah" in a garbled way.

"No. I mean it," he said. "Monty?"

"Yeah, okay." replied Montgomery.

"Cat?"

"What?" asked Cat.?

"You swear? No talking about this radio thing outside of our mountain."

"Yeah, I swear."

"Goldie?"

"I swear."

"Gehrig?"

"Yeah. Okay."

"Billy?"

"Yeah."

"Cannon?"

"What about to Gail?"

"Only if Gail can swear silence."

"Yeah, I guess so."

"Jack, Buddha, Sweet Bird?"

"Yeah." They said together.

"Pete?"

"Yeah. I swear."

"Last one. Dell?"

"Yeah. Okay. And I think we better keep a lid on this whole deal. Keep the broadcasts short, and move them around in frequencies and time. Don't do them at the same time each day. We don't want to give our LRDF guys more work."

"Okay, we got a deal," said Water Buffalo. 'Rogue Radio of Vietnam' is off and running."

"I'm gonna start putting together some music segments," said Buddha.

"Good," said Water Buffalo, "And I'm gonna start putting together news pieces we can talk about on the air. Anybody else have suggestions?"

"Yeah," said Dell. "I suggest we don't get busted."

"Aw, c'mon Dell, lighten up. This is gonna be our great adventure. This is gonna be great."

The second day, Water Buffalo talked with Pete about the mess that the Chicago Democratic convention had been, and how the kids across the country had been cheated by the political big wigs. The GIs were cheated too. The movement to end the war in Vietnam had been supported by a majority, but the candidates weren't going to end the war, they were going to continue it."

The talk was only three or four minutes. Then Buddha had a tape of both Janis Joplin songs and Jimi Hendrix songs that took about fifteen minutes. 'Piece of My Heart', 'The Wind Cries Mary', 'Foxey Lady' and 'Ball and Chain'. This time, there were dozens of comments on the air from soldiers with radios to 'Keep it going' and 'We're with you". They finished the broadcast with a quick talk about how supplies in Vietnam kept getting screwed up, and why should grunts on the line have to do without.

The third day, Water Buffalo talked with Monty and Buddha about the lousy music on AFVN. Then they played nearly thirty minutes of Rolling Stones, Beatles and Cream. When they finished the broadcast, they told their audience to 'keep an ear out'. It became their tag line.

Ten minutes after they went off the air, a voice came on the frequency and said it was "Rogue Two" and they started broadcasting Jimi Hendrix music with a little soul music as well. They stayed on the air for nearly thirty minutes.

On Day four, Water Buffalo interviewed Cat and Jack Wilson about time off between patrols and search missions, what it was like in the bush, and what it was like to stand down and relax and the use of drugs. Then Buddha had a thirty-minute tape of what he called California music: the Doors, the Beach Boys, Janis Joplin and Jimi Hendrix and a little of the Mothers of Invention.

When they left the air, saying "this is Rogue Radio of Vietnam, keep an ear out" and playing 'when the music's over, turn out the lights'. Within minutes another voice came on the frequency, claiming to be "Highland Harry" and playing more rock music. He was followed within another five minutes by "Rogue Two" for twenty five minutes, who was followed by "Country Jack", playing country music and talking about where to go on R and R.

The rest of the summer was Rogue Radio. There was very little serious searching for voice transmissions by the North Vietnamese. They produced one show each day, sometimes in the mornings, sometimes early evening. They continued to get comments on their show because it was a two-way radio, and enthusiastic listeners were encouraged to say something brief. It was clear they had found a niche. The soldiers all liked hearing hard rock, or peace-folk music, and many were turning more to the country style.

After three weeks there were more than a dozen free-lance radio shows on the soldiers' frequencies. They sprang up like weeds, with funny names, playing music that the soldiers wanted to hear, and commenting on the war, politics, and the goings on back in the states.

"You know, we started something, and now, maybe it's time we let it go, before trouble comes looking for us," said Dell.

"It was fun when we were the only ones out there. And it felt slightly dangerous to be doing that, kind of rebellious, but now I think you're right. We're just one of a dozen rogue radio shows… and we might be smart to stop before it goes too far and gets us in trouble," said Buddha. "And besides, we've played all my music at least two times and I don't have anything new to add."

Water Buffalo added, "If we stop, we can always come back if we think something ought to be said, about the elections or stuff going on in the states, but I think we've had our run too. This isn't easy to come up with a show every day."

"You know," said Pete, "I talked with Rocket the other day at Camp Eagle, and we're gonna have to take our R and Rs. He's talking about sending us two per week for the next six or seven weeks. They get in deep shit if they don't rotate everybody through an R and R. If you haven't put in a request, you better do it."

"Okay, just to make sure we agree, we're going to shut Rogue Radio down, and keep it down unless something big comes up," asked Water Buffalo.

"Yeah, right," they all mumbled. No one objected.

WHEN SAMMY CAME HOME

"Hey. You ready to go yet?" I called.

"I'm thinking about it. I mean, maybe I think I'll stay here, I'll let you pick him up, and then I'll be here when you get home." She didn't look too ready to go.

"Yeah. Okay, I guess." I said. "I thought you would be the first to meet him off the airplane.

"Well, I want you to do that. You know. You're his dad, and he always wanted to be like you. So you pick him up, and I'll be here when you get back."

"Ya' sure?"

"I don't know. I'll probably change my mind in five minutes"

"Well, I gotta go in the next five minutes… the one thing I won't do is be late."

"No. You go. I think tht will be better. Tell him I love him, but I want to see him here at the house."

I grabbed my jacket and an old snap brim hat. I always thought I looked like Indiana Jones with that hat. "I'll take the truck. He'll be glad to see that we still have it."

"Yeah, nice idea."

"Are the Robinsons going this afternoon?" I asked.

"I don't know. I would think so. Bobby's coming home with Sammy."

"They don't think much of the war. They may be making a statement."

"This is not a political rally. Our sons are coming home. Why in the hell would you not go to meet him at the airport and bring him home?"

"My only thought is that if Bobby needs a ride, maybe you can get all three of you in the truck. Give him a ride home."

"Yeah. Of course." I looked at my watch to check the time. I really had plenty of time, but I would rather be thirty minutes early than one minute late.

"What about Pogo?" she asked. "You could leave him in the truck. Sammy would probably be happy to see him."

"No. I thought about that too, but I think better to leave him here. Sammy will be happy to see him at our house… his house."

I gave her a hug, and a peck on the cheek. Time to go.

"You got a full tank?" she asked.

"Yeah, all set."

"Okay, give him my love."

"You bet."

After an extra hour's wait, the men of the brigade came marching up the runway from their landing area. Giant screens showed the men as they marched, and an announcer identified which platoons and companies were arriving first. The families' excitement grew as the men got closer and closer. Families met the men as they were dismissed to go on leave, and were making their way to the parking lots. Finally, Sammy's third platoon of the Delta Company was dismissed, and I met him walking across the runway. He put his arms around me, patting my shoulder blades.

"Sammy. Welcome home. How was your flight?"

"Happy. Happy to be coming home. Happy to be seeing you and Mom. Where's she at?" he asked, looking around.

"She decided to meet you back at the house."

"Oh," he looked decidedly unhappy. "Well, I'm glad to see you, Dad."

"Well, you gotta know how happy we are to have you home. A chance to get away from the war and get some rest."

"Dad, did you bring a car or a truck?"

"Yeah, sure."

"Well, a bunch of us decided we wanted to go over to the NCO club before we spread 0out in a hundred different directions. You know, 'the guys'. You probably did the same thing when you got home from Vietnam, didn't you?"

"Well, no, but we had a last night in Vietnam at the club in Saigon."

"Same, same. Can you get a ride home? I'll be home later."

"What about your Mother? Don't you want to see her?"

"Sure, Dad, sure. I'll see her tomorrow. Bobby's folks were going to meet him. Let's see if they can give you a ride, and then I'll take Bobby home."

Sammy didn't come home that evening, nor the next day. He was out with his friends, and they were drinking too much. Finally, Robinsons called to say that Bobby and Sammy were at their house, but neither one of them could drive. Would I come over and pick him up. I asked if the truck was there. They said no.

"Well, you had a celebration. I guess you had fun with your buddies."

"No. Not really, Dad." He said.

"Well, welcome home. We have a lot of catching up to do."

Sammy gave me a look. There was no mistaking it. I was treading on to a subject that he wasn't going to talk much about. "Yeah, well. How's Pogo?"

Pogo was our dog. He had been part of our family for six years. He was a mix of things, but mostly boxer, brown and white and a funny face.

Sammy was an infantry man. A grunt. A rifleman. He was part of a rifle squad, and more often than not, he was the guy who carried ammunition for the 50 mm machine gunner, the most powerful weapon in the squad. The machine gun was carried carefully, and used in squad patrols. Most of their patrols were through insurgent territory, and they had to be prepared to fire at any moment.

I thought back to how I felt when Sammy signed up. Mostly surprised. Sammy had been a straight guy growing up. Pretty good student, not exceptional, but he got his Bs and C-Pluses. He was a pretty good athlete. He made the football team, played basketball, and was a switch-hitting outfielder on the baseball team. He was well liked by the other guys, had lots of friends and seemed headed for a successful life.

Then, Sammy got the notion that he wanted to go into the army. Somehow, he thought that I would like that. I had served in Vietnam, although I never talked about it. I didn't discourage him, but I didn't encourage him either. I think I made it clear to him that there were dangers involved in warfare, I assumed he knew about that from his discussions with the recruiting guys. He wanted to be a good soldier. He wanted to do his part for his country and his home. I couldn't really tell him not to do that.

The Airborne Brigade trained and trained, small unit operations, fighting an insurgent enemy, watching your back… always, watching your back. They usually were driven out to a mission and spent weeks at an Operations Base. The base had numerous out stations, which were really just holes in the ground, maybe some netting to protect from mortars or grenades. The fighting was block by block, inner city street fighting.

I had always surmised that the fighting in Iraq was like the fighting had been in Vietnam. Small combat units, tight control, boring days walking through enemy controlled territory, and deadly nights when attacks could come at any time.

Sammy wanted to know about my experiences when he was young, but I didn't want to talk about them. I was afraid he would think fighting was glamorous… a good thing to do. I would have kept him out of the war if I could have. But, I didn't. I couldn't, when it came down to it.

"So, you want to talk about it?" I asked him. "You know, Iraq?"

"No, not really."

"Yeah, that's okay. I never wanted to talk about it either."

"I wish you had, Dad." He looked at his feet.

"Why? What do you mean?"

"I don't know. I was never prepared for the blood and gore."

"No one ever is…"

"I had four friends in my squad take hits on one patrol. We were just going next to a stream in a valley, we got slammed. Guys arms taken off at the elbow, legs blown off, chest wounds, gut wounds. Guys had no place to hide, just barren rocks and sand. And they never attacked us unless they had a pretty good numerical advantage and ground cover. Man, it was brutal."

I wanted him to continue talking. I knew it was probably good for him to get it out. I didn't say anything.

"Ya know what the Sarge said?" He asked. "We were lucky. We got all our guys onto medevacs and they saved their lives. Even if they now have to live with prosthetics for the rest of their lives."

"You made it through in one piece?"

"Yeah, and I feel like shit about that. Why me? More than half of our guys, our squad took hits of one kind or another. What did I do? I just happened to be in the right place at the right time. I feel lousy about that."

"But you're okay…"

"No one who fought over there will ever be okay. The question is, 'how the hell are we gonna live with it?' I don't know, Dad, I just don't know."

Sammy slept for a couple of days and nights. He didn't talk with anybody. He didn't go anywhere except around the yard with Pogo. Then the tremors and nightmares started. He was a handsome, well built young man. He could have been in the movies. He was still tan from his Iraq duty. And now, suddenly, he was pasty looking. His eyes were darting from one thing to another. He couldn't keep his hands still. And now his sleep was constantly interrupted.

In the night he would wake up crying out, or just crying. He was recalling ambushes and fire fights in Iraqi towns. Snipers were shooting his squad buddies, his friends. He would return fire with his machine gunner but then the machine gunner was dead too. There was no place to hide. He could only cry out for help.

After a week, the brigade initiated group counseling sessions for anyone who wanted to participate. He signed up. So did nearly everybody in his platoon.

"Dad, did you ever go to PTSD counseling?" Sammy asked him.

"No. They didn't offer that to us. In fact, the Army didn't even admit to Post Traumatic Stress as a problem covered by the V.A."

"Did they advise you guys how to handle battle stress?"

"No. They didn't admit it was a service related problem."

"Did you have the jitters and the nightmares and the battle memories and the return to battle scenes?"

"Yeah. I did. We just had to hope they would go away."

"Dad, I think I'm screwed for life. I don't see any way to get beyond this. Constant memories, fighting and blood, friends getting killed or blown up."

"Give this counseling a chance. Maybe it can work… don't give up on it yet."

"Dad, did any of your buddies die over there?"

"No. No one died, but six or seven came home early with severe wounds. A couple were taken to hospital ships in Danang harbor. It was a tough place to fight."

"Any of your friends do it when they got home? You know, suicide?"

"You know, I've wondered about that. I don't really know. Not that I know about. But I lost contact with most of the guys I was with in Vietnam. So, I don't really know for sure."

Sammy said, "You know what the army says? They say that twenty-two guys are taking their own lives every day. Twenty-two. That's a hell of a lot."

"Yeah. It is." I answered.

Two weeks later, Sammy returned to active duty in Fort Hood, Texas. His brigade was activated and would be re-deployed in eight to ten weeks. This time to Afghanistan. Sammy was glad to be back with the guys, sharing the work and the duty.

And then they heard about Bobby Robinson. Bobby shot himself in the yard at Fort Hood. Sammy and his parents trembled at the thought.

DANCING NAKED

DANCING NAKED

MOVING IMAGES

Elizabeth Taylor finished the seams on her <u>national velvet</u> pants,
snipped off the threads from the machine,
rewound the bobbin, pushed the threads to the back
where <u>Edward's scissor-hands</u> would not get tangled
in <u>charlotte's web</u>.
She folded the unfinished pants, then set them
on the small <u>separate table</u>
next to her sewing machine to be hemmed by hand later.
She slowly opened the <u>rear window</u> and
carefully climbed out to retrieve
her <u>cat on the hot tin roof.</u>
When Marlon Brando saw her there, he yelled,
"<u>Stella!</u> Are you out of your mind? What are you doing?
Leave the cat. It'll take care of itself. Get off there right now!
We have to catch a plane to <u>Dallas</u> today.
We'll never make it on time to the <u>airport</u>
if you don't climb down off your <u>ivory tower</u>.
none of that foolishness.
And be sure to close the window behind you because
<u>fools will rush in where angels fear to tread</u>."

She crawled back inside to take care of watering
her <u>man-in-the-moon marigolds</u> lest they dry out
while they were off on their <u>journey to the ends of the earth</u>.
They forgot about the cat, the heat of the day
and together they packed their incidental things,
checked last minute flight arrangements
and left in their <u>solid gold cadillac</u> for the <u>airport.</u>

DANCING NAKED

She was so nervous it took true grit to get her
to mount the stairway to paradise on this airplane.
She had listened to the news
about some snakes being transported.
It would take a witch-hunt and an exorcist
for her to be calmed for this exodus.
Be a brave heart, Stella, he encouraged.
It was her cousin Mildred Pierce whom they had planned
to visit over the Christmas holidays in Raintree County.
Thank goodness they were going south
because to have a white Christmas would
stall their plans and have them stay longer.
After she settled into her seat, she noticed
the birdman of Alcatraz next to her . . . a rude man who spit out
something about a Capital One Card.
Who was he? What nerve!
She pleaded with Marlon to switch seats.
She was no paper doll. He cared about her more than life itself.
It was up to him now to deal with the commercial traveler.
He could let it be, let it be, let it be, let it be.
She looked out the window
to the blue skies smiling at her,
hoped for a paper moon that night.
All was well.

DANCING NAKED

JO-HENRY'S DAY

Everyone forgets. Before you even think of it, remember this: she is not at all what you think she is. This is her story.

Born full grown in Manhattan, she had a hell of a time learning to manipulate the floors and walls of her tiny apartment. Her head and neck were often sore when she finally lay flat down at night on her Murphy bed. She had been cowering beneath the ceiling and doorways that led to the neighbors' apartments where she was finally able to stretch and relax. Tea every day at two was the dessert she delivered with her own clay croissant to Mrs. French.

Mrs. French never took that smirk off her face, always saying she was delighted with the company, but there was nothing that would erase the lines that told of her disappointment. Her neighbor was just too, too, she told her daughter on the phone often. They spoke every day at 8:30AM with no time for the daughter to speak her mind about the scuttlebutt that her mother blustered and fussed about.

Jo-henry was too tall. That was all there was to it. When she finally felt strong enough to venture outside without falling, her length would be stared at by everyone. Her fingers dragged on the ground, so they were filthy with the grime from the streets. when she passed by, people closed their windows. or turned on the fans that exuded fetid air away from their febreeze infested homes. (Thank goodness for the Johnson family-oriented fresh smell aromas. The choices were as many as the scent factories could concoct.)

Jo-henry loved the air . . . breathing forests, spring valleys, waterfalls and lavender fields. Nobody knew about Manhattan being the seat of such political sensitivities. Mr. Bigwig knew. That may have been why he lost the election. even Mr. Snotnose knew. He still speaks about the better part of sacred life in the big cities.

But I digress. This is about Jo-henry. Remember?
    She wandered through the streets, stopped at the playground with wishes to join the small children in their play. Her big feet tripped everyone and they shied away from her pleas.

    Approached one day by the rat who lived in the sewer, she had a talk with him. She knew he was a boy. Because of her height, he looked up to her, pleading for help with his team. This was not so easy as she could hardly hear him. Even his squeamish face that tilted toward her was vague. He murmured again and again that he needed help. His tail worked American Sign Language for his appeal. It took quite a while before she understood. The request was to join him. One tail did not easily signal a joint proposal. No wonder she was befuddled.

    Mrs. French opened her window and called out in almost a siren song to Jo-henry that tea was ready. "Toot-a-too" Was it already two? She made her apologies to the rat and disappeared behind a car, first yelling an echoing "boo-o-o-o-!" that startled the rat. She laughed. He was gone.

    The cloud of meandering dust was left behind as everyone suddenly poofed into mid-air. All that was left in the dust was a huge basketball. Instead of bending over to pick up the ball, she kicked it into the street. She had to get the cookies for tea.

    It took all of two jumps for her to enter the kitchen window where the two would sit and sip.

"How are things going for you today?" asked Mrs. French. "It took all morning for me to shred the tea leaves for your cup. I hope you like it. This morning, I thought about the sky and how perfectly blue it usually is. Today, it is not only gray, but there are sparkles that make it seems silver."

"Yes, I know. It's from the sprays that everyone uses. They turn the world around."

The ball stopped at the curb. There was no further that it could go. The force with which it hit the curb split the ball open. Inside, quite startled and not at all ready to face the world, was a small lamb, bleating a call that nobody in the area could understand. Particularly the rat who peaked out from his own small ball of mismatched netting and yarn. It was all that had kept him busy, fussing with this and that when nobody was around. What was he doing with it? Nobody knew but him. The lamb raised herself from the ball's insides and let out a wild bleating screech. 'What am I doing here?' he called out to anyone who would listen. It was Mayor Koch who was just passing through at that moment and thought he heard a sound . . . or maybe some guy named Giuliani. Something like that.

Mrs. French and Jo-henry also heard the sound and rushed to the same window where she could see the street, the same one as before. The view was perfect.

Scampering down the street was the lamb . . . and on its back was a shadow that they could not see very well. What was it?

It seemed that the opportunity for change and going home was there right in front of the rat. He grabbed onto the soft fur of the lamb, had hoisted himself into position with his front teeth biting the lamb's ear . . . not so tightly that he hurt the lamb much, (you would be relieved) but just enough to stay in position. His impressive tail worked as a rudder when they needed to make turns. (After all, the lamb was so young he was not yet able to know where he was going) At the same time, the clever rat sent out messages in sign language that they needed to be treated as notoriety. And they were.

Where was Jo-henry in this muddle? She had gone to the local police station No. 586 for help. No lamb should be left in the clutches of a rat. At the same time, Mrs. French was at the fire department. The men and women were just sitting down for their afternoon snack of cheesecake and bagels. (Remember, this is New York City!) They were laughing at something that the big one had said. It was difficult for Mrs. French to get a word in edge-wise, but of course she did.

"Help! We need help! Listen to me. We need help!" She stamped her feet. The men finally calmed down, swallowed the last of their meals, burped and looked up at the little grey-haired woman who stood before them.

They all rushed into the street just in time to see the lamb pass. One guy ran back inside to gather up his lasso. He had once lived in Texas. This surprised everyone and they spent a great deal of time watching him spin his loops while jumping lithely in and out. His partners whooped and hollered about the grace of old Bill long enough for their memory of why they were outside was gone. Even Mrs. French forgot. As she placed her hat back on her head, tilted it just to the right angle, not a right triangle, and adjusted the veil, she remembered that Jo-henry was once with her. Where had she gone?

The men returned to their spots at the dinner table while she disappeared into the direction of the police station. Ahhh. There was Jo-henry. She was laughing while looking through the album of all the notorious killers, wanted dead or alive.

"Come on, Jo-henry. We need to go back for our cups of tea." Mrs. French climbed Jo-henry's leg, just up to her knee and they went home.

"Now, what were we saying?" said Mrs. French to Jo-henry.

"MMMM" replied Jo-henry as she lifted her dainty cup.

They must have forgotten what they were doing. So did I!

A WALK IN THE PARK

Between the lovely old trees and the bandstand, Jo-henry and her squirrel pals scampered.

Because she was so tall, she could describe everything to the small critters who followed at her heels.

"This is the most wonderful park in the world," said she. "Winding pathways paved with rich, colorful autumn leaves."

Maples were always her favorite. The squirrels dug under piles and disappeared. Then chickadees emerged and called to each other. Moles scampered throughout the pathways that they had worked on all summer. One level down, a city below. Elegant, confounding sewers and culverts of their own making. Women and men with their children enthusiastically threw piles of color over each other, laughing all the time. Jo-henry sat on a couple of park benches and amusedly watched. Her uncle, Henry Williams (Roger's brother) for whom she was named, thrummed a diminuendo of piano notes that fell toward the crowd from the center of the bandstand. No doubt the keys had warped over the spring and summer rains. Now, autumn leaves were no longer, but he tried. She appreciated his effort.

DANCING NAKED

A chill passed by, enveloping her. she took three large steps to Bergdorf-Goodman's, avoided the plebeian Macy's, opened the door and yanked out the carpet runners to warm herself. People fell like Alice into her rabbit hole from losing their footings as she pulled. Cuddly wrapped in her new warm stole she ran fast away before the floor-walkers and guards could catch up with her. all they saw were some large feet standing still upon a nearby hill. It didn't dissuade them from their persistent search of the runner-thief. What were they thinking? Just another monument to the grand city. A fallen war hero. When they reached a swollen impasse, they solemnly returned to B-G's as they called their esteemed workplace, burdened by their fractured effort.

The two large feet slowly and stealthily edged away without anyone noticing. now she felt the warmth so much like the mink Mrs. French often sported to town. She imagined little rodents dripping from the tips of her curiously warm stole. They bit at one another as she smiled. Now that she was dressed appropriately, her direction was toward the Metropolitan Museum where she could show off her new duds at afternoon tea.

On her way, there was a huge crash. She looked up just in time to see falling from above a very large monkey. She looked up again and saw the side of the Empire State Building wide open to the wind. People were also falling. They sprinkled down like golden rainbows. Thankfully, they landed on his softness. She looked down at the horrendously large splat on the sidewalk. "Musta been a gorilla," murmured the subtleties from the crowd.

She turned away. The sight was unimaginable.

His legs were spread wide apart. His tummy had exploded. The stench was putrid. His arms also fell open. PEE-YOO! To walk around the beast took almost three hours, plowing through the awe of the growing crowds. Three hours of disgust, while the people who also fell brushed off the hair and cleaned themselves up to go back inside for work. Their noses were brilliant red from holding on too tight. The nose brightening became a contagious infestation like no other. Oh deer. And that was the beginning of the story of Rudolph.

By the way, just so you know, the guards were definitely fired. And Rudolph can be seen daily along with a brand new baby Nubian goat at the Central Park Zoo. No gorilla.

DELIGHT

Too-tall Jo-henry couldn't wait for her birthday. Each day she wrote those never-ending wish-lists for Mrs. French who lived next door. Mostly what she wanted were clothes that would fit her. The notes always sparkled bronze and chartreuse paper. These colors were appropriate to Mrs. French's background . . . she was French, you know. How could she be anything else? If she were German, she would be called Mrs. German . . . what if she we're Guatemalan? or Chinese? How about Indian? Oh, Jo-henry was glad to know just what she knew . . . and that was not much. She was not so good at schoolwork, and if the other countries were represented by Mrs. French, Jo-henry would never be able to figure out the colors. She would have to make up words. And Mrs. French would not be able to read the notes, for sure. This was all too silly! And terribly practical.

Her birthday was in March, coming soon. Besides clothes, her newest best present ever would be a little jumping frog. She dreamed of him or maybe her. Nothing would be better. She would have to slip the messages into the frilly saucer of the dainty teacup or under the greasy clay croissants. That would be a problem because she always spilled her tea and made a mess of everything.

She wandered through town to the edge of the Hudson River just before sundown on a very warm Sunday in February. There were some people watching the ferry leave for Staten Island, but not Jo-henry. A colorful ghost suddenly appeared just to startle her. When she jumped back, she fell into the arms of a fancy dan. His hat was feathered and so were his toes. She shielded her eyes from the sight, poking out over the shimmering water. Had he been there all along? As he stepped into the wet she looked up at a huge barge going by. A large sign on the barge's starboard side said: 'I WANT A LITTLE JUMPING FR…" but then it was gone. She was tall enough to see around the bend. Fancy Dan asked Jo-henry to read the message to him. "What do you think is the meaning of FR.?"

"Hmmm." Jo-henry mumbled something. And they both turned around to leave. This was a mountain too high to climb. Both were stumped as they wandered away so much shorter than they had ever been. Even too-tall Jo-henry. (Ooh, that mountain! Suddenly growing even higher!)

They thought and thought and thought some more.

"Ahh, I have an idea." said Fancy Dan. "Let's go to the library."

"What a wonderful idea, Fancy Dan. You are so smart. We can find out just what we need to know when we get there."

"You can call me Fancy. Everyone calls me that."

"Come on. Let's hurry before the library closes."

The guard at the library stopped them short. "HALT!"

Both Fancy Dan and Jo-henry saluted on the spot in reverence. "What could be the matter?"

"Don't you know? It is your feet! Or maybe it is your shoes. Whatever are they? Wherever are they? You cannot go into the library dressed like that."

They both look down at his feathery pointed toes. "Well, I cannot remove my feet" said Fancy Dan. "What shall I do?" This was quite a predicament.

After they wiped away their tears from the long sob, they huddled together on the steps and thought. Then they thought some more.

"Ahh, I have an idea," said Fancy Dan. Let's find some new shoes."

"What a wonderful idea, Fancy. You are so smart. I knew you would think up something."

New shoes? Platforms? Shiny silver New York shoes? Or coins to cover my feathers? He looked for the sunny side. Thank goodness there were two of them! Two friends, two feet. He covered them over with his jacket.

Back to the problem at hand . . . or foot. The sign. The library. Well, he brought the shoes to the all-knowing guard, tried them out for him, asking if it was okay. Would he let them into the library to find the meaning of FR? Unfortunately, the guard was too busy smoking a very long and smelly stogie. He wouldn't even look at Fancy who waited and waited and waited some more. Fancy was getting tired. He slid down into the planter by the front entrance and miserably curled up into his favorite ball. Finally he fell asleep. Right there on the steps of the library.

Poor Jo-henry. So alone. She waited for Dan to come back to her. When he didn't, she decided to go inside herself, for what else could she do. She wandered sideways through the stacks, hard as it was to fit in between. Thankfully, the ceilings were high enough for her to stretch herself to her full height. Ahhh! This was the place for her. In fact, she could see over the shelves into the next aisle. Her arms could stretch to five aisles over. "Wait until I tell Mrs. French!"

Below, it was very dark. A pinpointed lamplight shone on the desk toward a small man she decided must be the veritable librarian. He was almost the same size as Mrs. French, which made her feel comfortable. More comfortable than she already was. This was very nice, don't you think? She noted it in her Blackberry she kept in her back pocket.

She rested her long pointer finger on his desk, tapped it a few times with great massive thuds, asking for help. "Ahem!" (She had read that was the word to use.) The noise startled awake the librarian who said something with a snide expression that Jo-henry could not understand. Obviously, he had been pretending to read. The man stirred from his book, removed his sunglasses and looked up. His next words were "Howne0fcsdbasm" and "eotrbgh" (perhaps he was Guatemalan!) What could she do? There was a sign that interpreted the librarian's words.

"THIS WAY TO THE DICTIONARY"
What a relief. she followed the arrow until she found the dictionary. Opened it to the letter 'F.' Now to turn the tiny pages. They were delicate and hard to read because her clumsy long finger pointed to the page, covering its entirety. She lifted it, peeked beneath.

So slowly, Jo-henry squintedly mouthed the words, one after the other. When she got to the letters F with an R, finding nothing at all, there was nothing much else to do. Poor Jo-henry. Disappointed and dejected, she flew out of the library, angry and frustrated, slid down the steps, tripping over Fancy Dan.

Fancy had awakened in the uncomfortably hard granite planter to a wet discomfort. As a matter of fact, the squiggly things that bulged curiously in his pocket had annoyed him since his job at the Calaveras County Carnival. Just then, he tucked his hands in his pockets for what he was carrying all along. What he pulled out was quite a surprise for Jo-henry who was staring wide-eyed at him. There, in his palms, were two little jumping frogs. His great annoyance turned out to be her best gift. She jumped and hopped in glee. She could hardly contain herself.

"Oooh. you read my mind."

"Hmmm, why, yes I did. I always knew." He was so smart.

He placed them into the hands of Jo-henry and they laughed together, skipped and giggled their way all down 5th Avenue, past the shops, past Lincoln Center and there they parted. Fancy proudly returned to the river.

"Goodbye, Fancy Dan!…oops… Fancy… and then "Thank yooooo!!" She twirled her way back home on their tippy-toes.

There was no need to wait for her birthday or send notes to Mrs. French. Jo-henry had her best birthday present ever. Two of them!

LUMINOCITY

People scaled her long legs, using her leg hair to hoist themselves to a perch above all others, draping beads on every spot they could find, heading toward the orange-clouded sky until they reached her shoulders. From that platform they could reach her ears where they whispered with their groggy morning voices about the day. It was Mardi-Gras. She was annoyed at the repeated disturbance, but it was beyond her by this time.

The day was to become bright and glorious. Jazzy tunes played, warming up the early dawn. Trumpeters, drums, cornets and the good old slide trombone. Boolah! Bazzambi! And all the other notes on the digital scale. Women exposed their breasts in drunken brawls, comparing them to one another… none were satisfied… although the crowd cheered. Self-conscious were they. Jo-henry thought it was appalling. And so did I!

A parade of drummers stomped in rhythm down the main street, followed by many decorated and masked strangers. A hi-ho silver mounted police battalion followed. Whistle bands followed them. Jo-henry was inspired to play her own tune. She was absolutely tooty on her slide whistle as she fell into the formation. When the rest heard her, they separated and gave her enough room for those on the sidelines to rave their waves.

Flags of many visiting nations flew above the crowds… even one that proclaimed that the contingent was from Mars. The surprise was that it was not a planet at all, but the candy factory in Tennessee. A slide trombone (not the afore-mentioned) hit licks unknown to Brubeck and Armstrong. Historians took note.

A contingent of Girl Scouts from across the country had sailed on a barge down the mighty Mississippi to partake of the festivities. Jo-henry had never heard such twittering and giggling. They threw packs of 'thin mints' and 'peanut butter patties' to everyone on the sidelines. As quickly as they went into the air, they were caught by selfish sideliners. These girls were so tiny compared to her size that they stared uncomfortably at what seemed like a giant. Did Jo-henry notice? Not at all. She was busy downing cookies and dancing above the crowds.

Jo-henry laughed with gleeful cheer. She led a covenant of religious organizations, although she had no idea whether they were Baptist or Catholic or anything else. Because the Pope had recently given his resignation letter to the ever-never world, she was quite sure that the Catholics looked for any sort of new leader. Maybe she was to be the awesome ONE. She lowered her head in reverent prayer, although she was not sure what sort of prayer she could offer. It turned out to be a subliminally low rumble mumble. Those around her were observant and pleased that she had led them into a calm. Angels sang from the heavens, a sweet melodic tune. Should it have been Jo-henry's vocalization, the blast would have cleared the French Quarter.

Between the wine and beer, beignets and chocolate, Jo-henry was suddenly sick to her stomach. It was all too much. "Ooooh!" The pain was too much. "Ooooh!"

Wanting to remove herself from the melee, she stepped up to a lovely wrought iron balcony above the street, bending it under the strain of her weight, but thankfully it remained fastened to the sides of the stucco decor. She looked over the noisy city, happy and raucous and gleeful.

When she relaxed temporarily from the wild, she spied a casket of unstrung beads in the parade, reached down to gather them for herself. With her accumulation she showered the colorful beads down at intervals on the crowd as they looked up and celebrated her generosity.

Jo-henry was the star of the day.

DANCING NAKED

TORMENT

Since Jo-henry was so tall, everyone stared, although it was difficult for them sometimes to see up to her face. Her chin projected a screen from their view, blinding them as did the sun. Early morning hours were the best, just before dawn, but people who wished to speak with her needed to wait for cloudy days. And then the chance of conversation was definitely iffy. Megaphones were sold by the dozens outside of school. After a spate of sales, it became evident that they were to be distributed only to the teachers, and, of course, those social workers and advisers who dealt with Jo-henry during her school days.

Classmates were the most difficult entity in the environment. They would kick her, bumping into her toes to get her attention. Some would just walk by . . . well, around her. That is, if they had no business with her at the time. She sat on the floor at the back of the room with the bravest classmates climbing on her legs to see what was being written on the blackboard. Not only did her toes hurt from the repetitive sting, but also her shins and thighs became bruised from the unintentional abuse. However, she was pleased that the others were eager to be with her, even if they used her to see. After class and during recess it was she who wandered through the windows to the play yard below. When they bumped into her, they were unaware that it was Jo-henry herself. It could very well have been anything. "Oops!" they said, as they went on to play quite innocently, never looking back.

Others booed and hissed at their strange classmate. What could she do? The nattering pierced natural sounds of nature. The birds and squirrels that roamed the nearby trees kept her good company.

Thankfully, the children's noises seldom met up with her ears near the sky, maybe even in the clouds.

She wandered on her own time, oblivious to the shouts and curses from her classmates. Still, she was alone. Nobody for a friend except Mrs. French, who unfortunately could not follow her to school each day. It was against the rule. It made the children laugh and play to see Mrs. French at school. It certainly upset the applecart.

While the boys and girls were hustling to grab as many apples as they could fit into their pockets and pants, Jo-henry had sequestered herself as much as possible in the back corner of the schoolyard.

Although she felt that she was surely hidden from view, still the soles of her shoes and the length of her hair gave her secret hiding place away. She could have been a tree, for all they knew . . . or cared.

They jumped and hooped and hollered at her while circling as much as they could until it began to rain. All were getting wet, wishing they had umbrellas and rain hats. The downpour was very surprising. After all, there was never a forecaster who spoke of any impending storm. They were startled at the unexpected rain, thunder and even a bit of lightning.

They ran into the school once the rain began. The teachers rounded them up to file in an orderly fashion back inside into the assembly hall. As each found seats in an orderly fashion, the sounds of thunder roared from outside, louder than before. The sounds made them wonder if they should hide under their seats. Instead, they sat still as they could.

When the teachers called the role, all the children except Jo-henry answered with a cheery "Here!"

The question: Where was our girl?

They looked all over . . . especially in the little girls' bathroom where so often students were wont to hide. Nothing.

They called the Principal's office. But there was no Jo-henry there either.

Miss Take asked Peter Pickle to check the boys' room just in case. No Jo-henry.

What to do?

There she was, hiding in plain view. Nobody ever noticed. Nobody.

An all-points bulletin went up on the bulletin board outside the main office. The arts department developed a perfect design with lettering that was appropriate to everyone's doing the proper search. Teachers and students and even the secretaries and janitors signed off on the sign to say they had also been involved in the search. They vowed to stay in touch with one another while Jo-henry was missing . . . until she was found. Whistles were given out to everyone. Rattles, too. But there was never a resulting sound.

While all this was happening inside, the rain seemed to stop outside. In the sudden quiet, all were surprised and rushed to the windows, hoping for a rainbow, just as Jo-henry opened the schoolyard gates and disappeared down the street.

"There she is!"

"There she is!"

"There she goes!"

Her back was to the school, the administrators peeking outside. Nobody saw what was really happening. Jo-henry was soaked from crying so much. Her soggy, wet shoes slumped and stamped a thunderous recession from the school. It was not fair. She didn't know her value. She couldn't know.

Did she go back to the school? Actually, no. Mrs. French home-schooled her for the rest of the year.

While it took a bit of time for her to come down to earth, which you know is a long process, especially for too-tall Jo-henry, she eventually developed a wonderful combination of creative honoraria. She reached out to everyone, learning about them all, focusing on how they each had struggled with their own demons. Her days went sort of like this: well, you know so much about her days already. I've told you of her erstwhile adventures. Don't you remember? Check back with erst, please.

She went to school the next year with a new attitude. She kept her new best friend, Erst, in her pocket. Always. People wanted to know her, children and adults alike. Nobody was going to pick on her ever again.

FRIENDSHIP

Between the walls of the great house were many pathways to climb. Mr. Studley who is 16" on center plied the studs with lovely papers, scraps gathered from the bits of butter pats that fell in the waste basket in the kitchen of Jo-henry. (Jo-henry was a butter-lover.) They were perfect for the job because the glistening oil proposed a marriage for each and every one to adhere to one another. In fact, it was difficult to move one after the imposition was set. As a result, the papers were often thicker in some spots than in others. That became a wonderful roller-coaster of a ride as he slid from one area to another.

Sometimes, in the middle of the night, Jo-henry heard a sound that seemed like "Wheeeee!" It was only when all was quiet but the ticking of the clock and the sound of her breathing. Were the walls playing tricks on her? Or was it the wind that came through the cracks of the warped window frames?

She had read (she liked to read) that in the ear canal there were methods of sounds bouncing from one element to another as they proceeded to the brain. When those sounds finally registered in the brain, the airwaves made sense, became words, became cars going by, became cowboys riding horses, became leaves whispering in the trees. And then there may have been a game being played. That could well have been the resulting, "whee.' So many sounds did she remember and now thought about before she fell asleep. These were different. What could she tell about the slight variations that resembled "Wheeee!'?

She turned her head from one side to the other, closing off first one ear and then the other… this detective work was easily thrilled as she divided up the sounds, directing them from here to there.. or not there at all. Isolating the noises of her life was a challenge. It was the mysterious fun of getting to sleep. She realized her feet were in another room as they could never manage to accompany her head, although it was quite evident that they were attached to one another.

But getting back to the whee! Let's think about this.

Was it there yesterday? Or the day before?

Mr. Studley was having the time of his life, although his life was short. Ergo: this was the only time of his life. Actually, that is the only time of our own lives. When we live. Not that, but THIS. Enough of such deep thought. Back to our story. Have I lost you?

Mr. Studley was zipping through the walls, calling out in trills of whee and whooo (which sounded a lot like whee) until he was confronted by the spider who was living also in those walls.

DANCING NAKED

"Hey!"

"Hey! Stop right there! Whooo are you?"

Actually, the spider was saying, "Whoa!"

They both stopped. Stared at one another. It seemed like quite a long time.

"Hey! What are you doing? Who are you?"

"What business is it of yours?"

"Is that a way to speak with someone you do not know and have never been introduced to?"

"Don't ever end a sentence with a preposition if you would like to speak with me!"

"Okay, if you insist. Let's begin again." there was a pause while Mr. Studley decided about how to introduce himself. I would like to tell you a bit about me. Then he thought about that.

Why not just tell him or her his name and leave it at that? So he began again. "Good day. I would like to introduce myself. My name is Mr. Studley. Mr. Herman Studley, if you please. And to whom am I speaking?"

The spider wiggled her legs, batted at a bug caught in the web that hung between two studs. "Ahem." Clearing the horseness from her raspy throat. "I am Emily. You may call me Emmy. You may very well know me already. I am the prize given to actors and actresses each year. I am famous. .. and will be famous for a long, long time."

"Oh my goodness!" said Mr. Studley, gasping at the honor of such a grand acquaintance. It was clear that he was taken aback by this imposing personality. What else could he say? When he thought it over, he realized there was no problem because they were both in the same predicament, caught between the wood and a hard place. He smiled.

She rubbed her feet together, in silence. Smiled back at him.

There was something odd about their demeanors. Suddenly they were quiet. well, quiet enough to hear Jo-henry outside of the wall, but moving closer and closer.

"Shhh," they each signaled to one another by touching their one finger.. or paw.. or sticky wicket to their lips. They waited for a bit until they heard Jo-henry recede.

"We have to be careful"

"I agree" and they smiled again to one another.

"Wanna ride along my roller coaster?" asked Herman.

"Just as soon as I finish eating this bug, I would love to do that with you," replied Emmy.

Both listened with held breath for a bit more time. Jo-henry was gone.

In the quiet, Emmy smacked her lips, licked up the last of the slippery silverfish, climbed on Herman's back and they were off, down and along the steep and narrow pathways of the ride.

They enjoyed their friendship and the excitement of the buttery concourse.

If you listen closely, you may hear the same in your own walls . . . or not.

Most important: Do not wake Jo-henry, who finally became dreadfully bored and fell fast asleep.

DIVE

A summery hot August day in New York City. Everyone knows how brutal it can be. With enticing water everywhere to attempt cooling off, the suggested thought was to have some splashy fun. Got any ideas for the genuinely friendly and very sweaty Jo-henry? Is there a pool large enough?

"Well, I know about an ocean . . . or maybe Niagara Falls. No? This would be too scary. The roar, the rush, the fear would stop me. Let's think about this again. 'I can't' Not even a tiny bit from my large effort."

"What?"

A bar? A slammer? A cafe? With drinks? "I could never fit inside."

"You can't? Why not? Try anything."

There was a lengthy pause.

"Hey, What's happening?"

"I'm thinking. I'm thinking. Don't rush me." Gotta figure this one out.

Due to the huge difference in size, Jo-henry had to decide what to do if she was ever to join in the fun with friends.

You know, Jo-henry was as tall as anyone could imagine. The fact that she wanted to be part of the party became a huge conundrum to her. A puzzling puzzle each and every day, even many times during the day. A confounding puzzlement.

She thought. And thought . . . and then thought some more, looking at every which way she could join her friends. How could she be a friend if she stayed away from all their fun? She needed to think. Time passed. And passed.

She heard Lily and Frank whooping it up in the Center Cafe. A tear passed down her cheek. She straightened up to look at her reflection in the window of the Cafe, knowing the separation. All she could see was the image of her long scrawny legs, red and white striped socks and large tie shoes. She measured her shoes against the front door. They were large, too solid to fit inside, to enjoy their camaraderie. Pure frustration. She wanted in.

Then, a thought! She reached down. Ahhh, perfect! This is my answer. "How about my hand?" Her hand might just reach inside through the door.

"How about my hand? Let me try," she repeated. She pushed her hand through the door, remembering the American Sign Language tools she had learned from the dirty rat.

It worked! When her hand was inside, and signed a clever "HALLOOOO! in there" and "Hello!"

She waited. There! It was slow, but it was pleasingly effective.

What were they doing? No way to see them, she depended upon her hand signals.

Suddenly, "Oh, that tickles. Do it again. Ahhh. So calm to me in my palm. Just a small traverse along my lifeline. Ahhh." Unfortunately, nobody inside could read her.

She could not see anything, but felt the slow slippery slide of her friends climbing all in and between her fingers, tiptoeing along her palm, unably attempting signing. This all made her giggle.

Gurgling up from her innards, she almost forgot about the summer's severe heat. She pulled out her hand and reached into her pocket for her notepad. She wanted something to send into the Dive to her friends who were having fun, cooling themselves, drinking beers and fresh sodas while she was outside suffering.

The note: 'Please send me out something to drink, something cool. Please.' This was to be an engineering feat.

The note wriggled along the divide between her fingers and finally reached someone inside.

She waited. And sweated. And waited. And sweated.

In the same manner as the note was conveyed along the belt of her fingers, a very small cup of water passed outside to Jo-henry. It proved to be not even a sip. Quite unsatisfying. She gave up all hope.

She sat alone, thinking again. What would you do?

The cool harbor was one opportunity to escape the oppressive heat but the stinking sludge with grease and oil slicks from the massive ships in the channels stopped her.

The Falls at Niagara were becoming more and more enticing. Fear or not, summer was heading to her head, being as close as she was to the sun.

She turned right and headed north, over the roads and bridges on the turnpike northwest. It seemed all too enticing to enter the baths at Syracuse. However, she was hauled over by the police due to her causing too much of a stir and consequently a major traffic jam on the roads.

Film crews from many TV stations were out en masse to catch sight of Jo-henry. So unfair as she was only looking for calm and cool.

The Mayor came out to calm the communities.

The Supreme Court met to amend all amendments relating to the entitlements of personal space.

The President was called in to bluff his way through another erudite speech.

Everyone across the country clapped and cheered at his openness. When given the opportunity to ask questions of the esteemed being, the press was dumbfounded to silence. The resounding un-thunder sent them back to their limousines and offices and the six o'clock news was frighteningly silent.

Jo-henry moved on.

DANCING NAKED

At the border of Canada, there was nobody to check her credentials. (all were calling cable companies and internet providers, Twitter and Facebook accounts to protest the lack of news.) A small group of bagpipers shorted out a honking tune. She passed by.

Turning southwest once again, she smelled the fresh and quite dazzling air at the other end of the St. Lawrence Seaway. Her direction was perfection.

Those tourists who stood at the edge of the Falls, with bus drivers carefully scanning all watches and clocks to hurry their fares back to the next stop, were aghast at the approach of Jo-henry, who smiled at the chance of tumbling into the fresh mist and final pool. She stripped off her colossal clothes, folded and lay them on the fence rail that protected the little people from tumbling into the Falls. Then, in her altogether, she stood with a Cheshire smile and tipped herself into the cool breath of refreshment. There were resounding screams from those at the sight, those who had not yet boarded their buses; a wild stampede raced toward the edge. Unfortunately, the massive pushing and shoving to see the fall into the Falls drove more than a few others over the edge. The noise was hardly audible from all concerned.

Smilingly spirited and happily refreshed, Jo-henry brushed her curly hair from her eyes, reached upward and caught each tourist in her empty palms, replacing them at the top where they proceeded to their outward transportation. At last, Jo-henry was thrilled to help.

As they all drove away, putting away their cameras and postcards, there was nothing but the roar of the Falls and the sound of her joyful, refreshed laughter.

DANCING NAKED

MELODY

Toot-too-tootle-oo-toot-too!

What was that? Maybe you know.

She fell into the tuba and blasted a 'woo-woo-zoh!' for the crowd who clapped and raved about the fete that accounted for the many sounds that occurred at noon and midnight each day. They didn't know. Did you?

As she made her way through the valves and stems, she exited her ride and soon entered the clarinet. The tune carried her sublimely from one to the other. That was a lot easier, following one long slide into the bwah-zzz-boo-bwaaah of the brilliant brass trombone. Her ride was more than fun. "Whee" she exclaimed melodically to everyone on the sidelines. How could she stop? Then the oboe sounded, but the turns were tough enough that she also became stuck at the mouthpiece. She looked into the distance, reached for a drumstick and found Johnny-one-note. He was definitely caught inside and had been crying.

"How long have you been here?" she asked him.

"That is a queer query. What makes you ask?"

Hmmm.

"I mean, why are you asking me anything when you are inside, too. You must already know what it is like to be stuck, stuck, stuck, stuck, stu...."

"Yes I know. Because of my size I become all too often quite amazingly stalled in quite obscure places." Quite. "But wait! Hold on there. I was not thinking you ware wanting to be inside. Why and when did you come?"

"I have been here since the oboe vacated his seat. He ran off with a reed and has not returned."

"How long ago was that?"

"Hell (oops, I am not supposed to say that!) if I know. Warm here, isn't it? Getting hotter every minute. Ouch! Ouch!"

She followed his painful gaze. They both looked down at his feet.

"What's going on in your feet?"

"Burning up!" (that proves it!)

"Well, stay away from me, willya! What did you say your name was? Willya?"

"No. My name is Johnny. I can't sing anything but high C." There was a long and winding pause. And that was all he said.

There was a long interval of no sound and hardly any sign of breath. And then….

Johnny insisted on this name, although nobody responded when he spoke. His answer to everything was a screeching high "C", so not a soul could understand him. Nobody but Jo-henry. She became invaluable to the story, so much so that we all had to wait until she squeezed herself from the instrument to tell us all of a plan she had cooked up with her committee. Her committee of one.

"Well. Jo-henry, what are your plans?" he called from inside.

"Not to be too secretive, I am going to call my oom pa-pa.?

"Yes, and then what?" he answered eagerly, almost breathlessly. This was his chance to escape.

"What what?"

"That's what I said. What."

"Your oom pa-pa?"

"He's the only father I have had and will ever have, I hope."

"What do you call him?"

"I name him Oom. Sometimes I find him when I need calm. When life gets too busy, I say, 'Oom' or 'Om.' It calms me further."

After the excision by Oom-pa-pa. (he dislodged the reed that had become stuck at the mouthpiece.) Johnny slithered out in a snarled convoluted crescendo, baying an eerie, monstrous succession of tones, quite unlike anything Beethoven or Mozart had ever composed. As they untangled themselves, settled themselves, they looked at one another, saw that they were as long and winding as snakes, enjoying their now stylish figures, admiring each other. An unlikely pair. Life was good, better than they had ever expected. In tune, finally.

DANCE

"May I have this?"

"What did you say?"

"May I have?"

"I need you to bend down to meet me. I can hardly hear you."

"May I please…..?"

Spirit comes forth in a demure pavane or a graceful waltz. But are you the one who wants to take this step into the future?

"Can we meet somewhere in the middle?"

"A slight reach for me."

"And a huge grab for me."

"You have been my sweetness. We need music."

"What else can we do?"

The band strikes its first note. Music falls at their feet. If one were to take one step, how many would the other need to keep up? Mathematics. Can you figure this out? One long, fourteen short. Divisive division.

"Help me."
"I will. I'd be honored."
"One step, then another.."
"Puff puff. I am having a hard time."
"I am hanging on to your shoelaces… Should I get tired from trailing you, do you mind if I jump right up on top of your toes? Would I hurt you? I don't want to do that."
"Two steps and there I fly delightedly into the stratosphere."

A sole soul grabbing your soles, hoisting myself to the half step, over your instep, slowing the beat to keep down with us. Inching upward, ever onward, the gentle cadence offers romance and titillating joy.

"Sincerely, I wish to slide away with you into the stardust. Though I dream in vain, in my heart it will remain the simple glide across the floor into the memory of this sweet refrain."

"MMMMMMMM" (Come on, tell me true. Are you dancing with me?)

"mmmmmmmmmmmmmmmmmmmmmmmmmmmmmmmm"

BOREDOM

It was difficult enough to be Jo-henry, but to think beyond the issues at hand was something that dragged on and on in her mind.

First there was the thumb… That's one. Upside down. Downside up. Curious. How many joints could she count? Of all the joints . . . well, let's not go there. And what possible reason could there be for this enterprise? Blah blah blah. Discount that effort. Please. Joints. Please.

How many joints had she been in with those who were just as reliable as she with the same connective tissue that allowed her (like the great apes and minor monkeys) to handle her hand. (Thank you, Dian.) The question furthermore: what would the four other fingers represent in the scheme of things had the accompanying digit been left behind? (Perhaps the entire alphabet.) Imagine the impossibility (huh?) of reaching and grabbing and sewing and pinching without the use of the elegant thumb. Ghastly appendage on its own, hanging handily from the side.

What do you think?

She tapped her fidgety digits handily against her cheek, feeling the spatter of rain as if it were raining. Lines for life . . . as it goes by.

Nails rigidly nailed into the end of each finger and thumb give nobody a true purpose in dealing effectively with them. Why name them differently? Emery spoke up, quietly pointing to goals. Decorate me as I am none other than the shell that protrudes from its finality. Scratch, sniff, point and go. What more? Hum. Ho.

"Shall I nap?" or "Stare out the window, between my digits, deciding what and how to introduce one to the other. Seal them together and they mean less . . . or more." Yawn. It's no wonder that tattoos decorate knuckles. We take it all for granted. Count them again.

Her eyes became bleary. Go ahead. Count them.

Ahhh. Shadows on the wall. Dancing dully. Spiraling inward and toward themselves, in mobius direction they fly. Jo-henry offered up the chance for them to soar. Then recoiled into a small fistful of compressed air. Ah, perfection. That's the punch line.

Begin at the beginning. Touching one index finger to the other in a gentle arch, the form is not even a second long before a train skims across the newly formed bridge. She counts twenty-two cars before the caboose which is bright red as usual.

There was a tiny woman waving from that platform. "Halloooo!" She squints to see more perfectly who it is. Is it someone who needs help? She quiets her mind to hear a distant "halloooo."

Someone she knows?

She wants to reach for the woman who now seems to be asking to be saved from this growling train. However, if she does, the bridge on which the train travels would crumble and many more passengers, conductors and engineers that hold the train together would be killed. A crystal clear 'Hellllp!' clearly calls to her. With all the mysterious hubbub, she wonders. Does this one person know how precarious the situation? She looks more closely. And can hardly believe her eyes when the small woman begins yelling again to her: "Jo-henry! Jo-henry! It's me! Mrs. French! Can you see me?!"

Just before it was to disappear into the tunnel, Jo-henry slows the train with her left pinky, careful not to upset the bridge., careful to not cause a wild and frighteningly disastrous rattle and crash of cars into the river below. As the train safely disappears into the tunnel and is almost gone, Jo-henry realizes she can now disassemble the bridge, after picking her good old friend, Mr. French from the last train car with delicate removal. She sticks out her tongue and Mrs. French desperately and courageously hops on. "Be careful! Do not swallow me! I am your friend. Don't you remember me?"

Jo-henry wipes her clean, sets her on her lap and gives her a very careful and much appreciating big hug. They sit together once more in happy remembrance.

Mrs. French lifts a lovely aromatic croissant from her apron pocket to share with Jo-henry. The two friends relax with broad smiles as they both look off into the distance. The taste is sweet.

DANCING NAKED

Yawn.

And with that, the day is over.

"Been quite a day," as she wiped the sweet strawberry jam from her chin.

"I'd say so!" said Mrs. French, looking out across the sound.

Don't you agree?

THE END

DANCING NAKED

RETRIBUTION

Kait punched two on her speed dial and leaned back against the building. Warm sunshine fell on her upturned face. Air laced with bus exhaust was a welcome change from corridors scented by antiseptic cleaning fluids and chemical deodorizers that soured, not covered, the odors of urine and decay.

One, two, three rings. She closed her eyes and sighed. He wasn't going to answer.

Then a click and a breathless, "Hello."

Kait allowed her tense body to sag against the scratchy red brick. Was the warmth from hearing his voice or the sun warmed rock?

"Hey," she replied softly, trying to erase the relief from her voice.

"Hold on. Give me a minute to get outside where I can hear you." The background sound of chattering voices receded, replaced by the echo of footsteps in a corridor, the whoosh of an opening door, then unexpectedly, the call of a cardinal.

When he came back on the line, Kait said, "It must be beautiful there. I can hear the birds. How did your presentation go?"

"They laughed at my sorry jokes, nobody fell asleep when I droned on past the hour, and there were a slew of questions during Q & A."

"I told you not to worry, that you'd wow them." She asked, "Does it look promising for the new research grant?"

"The team thinks so. If things go this well the next couple of days, we'll be in good shape." His voice dropped a notch, lower, more intimate, "What's wrong? Did he die?"

"No. I just wanted to talk to you," Kait answered a little too quickly, unable to keep the hint of desperation out of her voice.

Silence from the other end of the line. He knew her so well. He would wait for the truth to come tumbling out of her mouth.

She could hang up.

She wouldn't.

He knew that, too.

"The doctors have suggested disconnecting the life support and letting him go."

"What does he say about that?"

Now the words tumbled over themselves. "He can't talk. The second stroke paralyzed him. He barely responds." She took a deep breath, "Why me? Why didn't he assign Mom as his health care proxy? He didn't say anything about it, tell me what his wishes are. He's my mother's father, but I barely know him." Her voice rose to a near wail as the words continued to spill out, "How can I say, 'Turn off the machines, kill my grandfather'?"

"What does your mom say?"

With the phone in a white knuckle grip, Kait paced back and forth on the uneven sidewalk. The sun was too bright here. A headache pulsed at her temples and sweat cut a jagged path down high cheek bones made pale by stress and lack of sleep.

"Mom? I quote directly. 'I'm not coming home from Spain. Let the old bastard wallow in his own piss.' I don't understand her, Brad. After Mom married Sam she changed. She barely speaks to her own father now. Why? What happened between them?"

"Have you asked her?"

"Oh, yeah."

"And?"

"She does one of those vague hand wave things and changes the subject."

After a pause, Brad asked, "Do you want me to come home, honey?"

Taking a deep breath and expelling it on a sigh, Kait answered, "No, the seminar is too important. It affects the funding for your whole team and research that will save lives."

"I don't like it, but you're right." The crunch of gravel under his size elevens underscored his frustration with the distance between them. "Is Joss still there? Can she help you make a decision?"

A smile lightened Kait's face. "She took Jannie to pick out a birthday cake. They were arguing over whether to put the number eight on it, princesses, or snakes."

A chuckle echoed down the line, "I'm betting your sister was voting for princesses, and our daughter campaigning for reptiles."

"Got it in one. How do I have a daughter fascinated by creepy crawlies? I hate them." After an involuntary shiver and brief hesitation, Kait continued, "Joss thinks the world of grandfather. She always comes and stays over when he's in town. We'll talk."

"Gotta go. The next presentation is due to start. Call you tonight." Brisk footsteps and the whoosh of the door as he disconnected echoed on the line.

As Kait stepped off the elevator, Joss exited from their grandfather's room. "I dropped Jannie off at your neighbors."

"Thanks. Is grandfather better?"

"No, why?" Joss replied.

With a shoulder shrug, Kait answered, "No reason, I guess. It just looked like a smile on your face. I thought maybe he responded, was talking."

The sisters entered the hospital room and talking quietly settled in chairs by the window. "The doctors want me to make a decision about discontinuing life support, that it's the most humane thing to do." Kait hesitated briefly then continued, "He's still there, Joss. I can see it in his eyes. His mind is working even if his body isn't."

"I agree." Joss's voice was even, emotionless.

Kait massaged her red rimmed eyes. "Maybe they're right. Would it end his suffering, allow him to die with dignity?"

She resisted the urge to pace, instead rising and moving to stand by the old man's bed. Purple veins spidered under thin skin almost as white as the bed sheets. His eyes were closed, crepe skin hanging lax on bones that looked too frail to support anything heavier. "Why is Mom so angry with him?"

The question hung in the air.

Joss's entire body sagged then stiffened. Her head came up, her spine straightened, and her eyes narrowed.

Almost under her breath Kait hissed, "You know. You know what happened. Tell me! When Mom married Sam, things changed. What happened?"

In an atonal voice, Joss began speaking "Sam is a child psychologist. He's trained to recognize abuse." Joss shivered as though shaking off a heavy coat. With a glare and anger twisting her features she turned on her sister, "Didn't you ever wonder why when grandfather visits I always come and sleep in Jannie's room instead of on the couch in the family room?"

Struggling to understand what wasn't being said, Kait shook her head.

Joss strode to the bed and roughly shook the old man's frail shoulder, "Open your eyes you filthy pervert." When watery eyes blinked open she continued, "I wasn't willing to try to prosecute you after all these years, but I saw the hunger in your eyes when you looked at Jannie. There was no way you were going to victimize my niece the way you did me."

She turned to Kait, "I made sure Jannie was never alone with him and told the sicko bastard that if he even touched her, I'd stab his eyes out with a scissors and then use them to cut off his dick."

She glared at the shrunken figure on the bed. "I was kind of hoping you'd try, old man. I would have enjoyed doing it."

Looking down at the frail figure and spoke, "You hate being a vegetable don't you, you bastard? How does it feel to be helpless, out of control of your own body? I can do anything I want to you, and you're the victim now.

With a smile that wasn't a smile Joss turned to Kait and said, "I think you should leave him on life support." She left the room.

Three nights later, Kait nestled her cheek against Brad's shoulder. The volume was muted on the television, its flickering screen the only light in the room. Brad twisted a strand of her hair around his finger as he asked, "Have you decided whether to take the old man off life support?"

Kait answered with a brief shake of her head, "Joss visits him every day. I don't know what she says, what she does, but when she comes out of his room she has that scary smile on her face."

A sob broke in Kait's throat. In words that tumbled over themselves she asked, "What kind of sister am I that I didn't know what was going on? That when we were kids he sexually abused

Joss whenever he came to our house, and I had no clue? Why didn't she tell me?"

After a long silence, in a voice barely more than a whisper, Kait added, "Joss came today to help pack up his things."

When she didn't continue, Brad asked, "And?"

While I boxed his clothes for storage, Joss bagged his medicine to take to one of those disposal places.

Kait drew away and wrapped her arms around herself, averting her eyes to stare at the silent T.V. screen.

"There's more," Brad prompted.

A single tear slipped down her cheek as Kait pulled her legs up to her chest wrapping her arms around them, lowering her forehead to rest on her knees. In a muffled voice she said, "Joss slipped one bottle, the blood pressure prescription she just filled for him, out of the bag, went in the bathroom, and shut the door. The toilet flushed, and she came out without it.

"She had that same half smile that she gets after she's been alone with grandfather. Then she made that motion you use when you're dusting something nasty off your hands and said, "That's done. Jannie, all of us are safe."

"I felt so guilty, checking on her, but after she left I looked in the bathroom. The empty bottle was in the wastebasket."

Hesitating, Brad asked, "You think she changed the . . ?"

Kait cut him off not wanting to hear the accusation actually spoken, "No! No. The meds, I don't know." Kait slapped her hands over her mouth as tears spilled down her cheeks.

In a thoughtful voice Brad mused, "Your big sister loves you and Jannie more than anything. She protected you from his abuse as a child and is just as loyal to Jannie,"

Kait raised tear glazed eyes to his as she asked, "What should I do?"

Brad pulled her close, resting his chin on the top of her head. She felt the comforting rumble in his chest as he finally asked, "What do you want to do?"

Without hesitation Kait replied, "Love Joss even half of much as she loves me."

DANCING NAKED

SITTING DUCKS

Alex and I spend most of our time in the dog house, but a few years back we finally found something our wives whole-heartedly supported; namely, fishing for striped bass in late September.

This was the fall run, when schools of Striped Bass made up in the shallows around Cape Cod for their southerly migrations. During these years of plenty, no one at the time thought there would ever be a shortage of this species. In a good afternoon, Alex and I could haul in a week's pay, and as long as we agreed to split it fifty/fifty with the you-know-whos, we received no complaints whatsoever.

Now, while some people might not perceive this as quite fair, we, on the other hand thought it sounded like the best bargain we'd run across since the time we got paid to taste ice cream . . . but that's another story.

This was to be our our duck-camp money. Our mad money. Without the slightest twinge of guilt, we could spend our half on any fool thing that struck our fancy.

That's when we bought the decoys.

I assure you, these weren't your regular run-of-the-mill decoys. They weren't even magnums. These were special.

We got the idea when we were out bass fishing, watching sea ducks--flock upon flock of them--skimming the wave tops. There were Butterball Coot, Old Squaw, Surf Scoters and Eider Duck by the hundreds. We spent as much time watching the birds fly by as we did counting our mounting fortunes.

Hauling in fish, mind you, was always one of our most favorite things to do, but it couldn't hold a candle to a day on the marsh, hunkered down--just barely out of the weather--in a duck blind. So, as we caught our finny treasure, we'd naturally talk duck stories.

Well, anyway, we saw all these birds and figured we'd stumbled upon a long lost secret. We knew people hunted these ducks in the days of market-gunners. We'd read the stories, and talked to the old-timers who claimed they remembered fathers and uncles that had shot thousands for the big city food merchants. They even talked about dealers who would come down from Boston on the train every day, to buy direct from the hunters.

In our minds, Alex and I felt that anything pursued that attentively, harvested that heavily, and sold on the open market for real money just had to have an interest for us. Besides, there were thousands of them flying around out there.

We decided nothing else would do, but that we had to stop and talk to one of these old characters and satisfy our curiosity. This would have to be handled delicately, without sounding too interested, you understand. Then, just maybe, we'd learn how to go about this business the easy way.

To make a long story short, our chosen mentor--a local named Chester--loved to talk about the old days. He even offered to sell us a full set of coot decoys all rigged and ready to go.

He dragged us out back and pointed to a barn that was a few score years older than he was, and just as gray. Half falling down, it was so tired that it had to be propped up by boards wedged against the sides and door. He explained that the decoys were buried under a pile of other treasures in the back of the building. If we were willing to "clean out the shed" and put in some new corner posts, he thought he just might part with the thirty 'coys for a hundred dollars. Then, just to sweeten the pie a little, he said if we found anything else we wanted, he'd throw that in too.

Eyes gleaming with a mixture of greed and guilt, Alex and I told him we couldn't do that, but if we came across any real finds we'd make him an offer. In his old-fashioned way, he insisted that wasn't necessary, and that we should shake hands on a good deal for all of us.

Formalities completed, Chester told us to, "Have at it, Boys!"

Chester did have one more request. He went on to explain that before he left this earth he had a hankering for just one more, old-fashioned, game supper: one like his mother used to cook.

So we promised him that if we got any Butter Ball coot, we'd give him a "mess" and join him and his wife for an old-time sea bird stew.

Hey, what could we say? This was a dream come true. Not only did we have someone to provide the equipment, and teach us the finer points of hunting birds, but he was going to cook them for us too.

Still feeling a little guilty about the price we'd agreed on for thirty decoys, and not wanting to seem too eager to dig into that vault of discarded booty, we told him we'd be back the next Saturday.

When that appointed day finally arrived, Alex and I wheeled into Chester's yard bright and early. There he sat on the steps waiting for us, with a great big grin on his crinkly-eyed face.

In a grand flourish and cloud of dust, we backed Alex's truck up to the door of that big old shed, and promptly slammed into the prop that was holding the door shut.

This newly-created, flying missile exploded through the shed door's window in a shower of glass.

Right then, something should have told us this just wasn't going to be our day.

As far back as I can remember, Chester had always been an old, scrawny, stoop-shouldered, crotchety, little-bantam-rooster-just-looking-for-a-fight kinda guy. So, when he heard that glass breaking, he was out back there before we could even get the pick-up's doors open to survey the damage.

"Damn fool showoffs!" he was hollering. "You look'a here boys, that-there deal didn't include no broken glass! I 'spect now you're a'gonna haft'a fix that-there broken door, a'fore you haul all a them there dee-coys away, ain'tcha?"

Red-faced, and full of humility and apologies, we answered a collective, "Yessir!" All the while thanking our supposedly lucky stars we hadn't knocked the whole cussed building down while we were at it. (Little did we know at the time, that such an event was a physical impossibility.)

Needless to say, we went right to work after our initial faux pas. We moved the offending vehicle, propped the doors open, and stopped dead in our tracks.

Staring in utter disbelief, we discovered the whole building was so full there wasn't room for dust! Floor to ceiling, wall to wall, I don't know how he ever got the doors shut to begin with.

Taken aback, and still a little chagrined by our window incident, we figured a deal was a deal, so we started filling Alex's truck.

Out came old rubber boots that had been vulcanized to each other by many, many summer suns of melting in that hot shed. Canvas tarps, or were they square-rigger sails? Feather pillows that must have been made from Dodo birds. Mile upon mile of rope, any size you can think of, including some as big as my arm, and all of it so rotten it fell apart when we picked it up. Mixed in with this were broken tools of every description. Shovels, axe heads, clamming hoes, rakes, eel spears, scythes, and wheeled hand-cultivators. Broken bushel baskets, galvanized buckets, and wash tubs whose bottoms you could see daylight through. Kegs of mixed nails (the bottoms of which dropped out as soon as we picked them up), cranberry scoops, pitchforks, on and on, ad infinitum.

Some of the stacks of trash were so alive and crawling with six and eight-legged creatures we thought of calling a local entomologist to see if we had discovered some new pests.

The moldy air--most of which seemed to be a mixture of rope-fiber, feathers, and dust--was full of the aroma of naphtha, given off by tarred fishing-gear. Mixed in was the distinctive smell of long dead rodents and their sundry droppings.

To finish this mental picture, I have to include the din of Chester's old hound Harry doing his best to deafen, or scare off any life forms who might be stupid enough to remain in residence.

Ah yes, and then there was Chester. Chester stood by all this while, and directed our sweaty labors. He was pointing out and giving us a running history lesson of where every single article came from as he orchestrated the resting place of each piece among the various mountains we were building.

We had long since filled the pickup to overflowing, and were now just sorting to piles of "throw away," "maybe throw away," "maybe keep," "definitely keep," and possibly things he might sell if someone were to make him a reasonable offer.

I was beginning to see that the distinction between which pile an article went into was decided upon more by the value Chester had placed on the memory it evoked, than by its material worth.

We didn't care what other treasures he wanted to sell. Here it was noon, and we were looking at six or seven trips to the dump--minimum--and we still hadn't gotten down to the level the decoys were supposed to be on.

By now, we wouldn't have given him a dollar for the whole building. Alex and I hadn't figured out how he'd gotten us to pay him $100 for the privilege of cleaning out his barn in the first place, so we were sure that any new offer would be more than we could afford.

After a quick stop at a local lunch counter, and the nearest dispenser of liquid dust chaser, we made our first trip to the dump. While we were eating, we determined that if we were ever going to finish this project we had to distract the old man while we got rid of all that stuff we were hauling out.

Scratching our heads a little, Alex hit upon the answer. When we returned, we brought him back a little bottle of brandy. We suggested to him that it was to help make his day go a little easier. You'd have thought we'd brought him the moon. He sidled off around the corner of the shed, where his wife wouldn't catch him, and had a sip or two. Wiping his chin with his sleeve, he proclaimed it the best "hooch" he'd had in years.

By the time we got back from our second trip to the dump, he was sitting, leaning against the shady side of the building. He told us what a wonderful job we were doing, and what great boys we were to help an old man out like this.

After the third trip, he was laying there with his arm wrapped around Harry, and singing some old sea chantey at the top of his voice, oblivious to our presence.

Wouldn't you know it? Along about this time, his wife came tearing out of the house, breathing both fire and smoke.

Chester sobered up on the instant and scrambled to his feet. Stuttering and stammering, he told her we'd found an old bottle of rum-runner brandy in the shed, tucked away all these years since prohibition. He tried to explain he'd just been "sampling it" to make sure it was safe, before he gave it to "them-there boys," nodding in our direction.

Figuring we were all in cahoots, Sarah gave us a look that would have melted lead, and marched him off to the house.

As he stumbled by, he gave us a wink that would have done a minstrel show proud.

We wasted no time throwing the rest of the stuff outside, letting it fall wherever it may.

Finally, after a few scares from moldy, rotted, cloth-bag decoys, we got down to the ones we had been working so hard for.

All they turned out to be were pairs of silhouettes made of three-quarter inch stock, and nailed to each end of a piece of strapping. Each strapping was a little longer than the last one, so when you piled them up they nested together in a neat stack. We strung one batch of them out on the floor, and found the slats were rigged parallel to each other, so they looked like some strange sort of rope ladder. It was obviously a great way to carry them and an easy way to deploy them.

Clever, these old timers.

The silhouettes themselves were just painted flat black with a spot of white behind each head.

The anchors were certainly impressive. Judging from the obverse, they'd been molded in a wooden salad bowl. Cast from lead, they weighed about ten pounds apiece, and there must have been a hundred feet of tarred cod-line on each one.

After counting them, we discovered there were thirty pair of decoys, strung ten pair to a nest instead of thirty in total as we had thought. Not completely trusting old Chester's intent, we decided to leave them right where they were until he was feeling himself again. Then he could spell it out for us. Besides, we didn't want to offend him until we knew for sure "how to set up proper" for these birds.

We lugged everything we felt was worth saving back into the shed, and then made four more trips to the dump to wind up our day.

Begrimed and bedraggled, we stopped by his house and told his wife we'd be back in a day or two to talk to Chester about the decoys. Then we took off before she could tell us what else we could do.

A couple of days later, while we were stiffening the shed so it would stand alone, Chester--looking a little sheepish--came out and confirmed the whole lot was ours.

DANCING NAKED

We paid the man, even though by now we were rather certain that these old-timers were clever about more things than just decoy rigs.

Business over, he sat down on an upturned bucket, and drew in the sand with a stick how we should set-up our "shadow deecoys." He suggested we place the three strings in a triangle, with the base towards the shore, then stick our dory between the two shore-side batches.

Interrupting him, we told him proudly that we didn't use a dory. We had a modern fiberglass runabout.

He shook his head and, looking very somber, told us how sorry he was about our misfortune. "A dory at anchor" he said, "would ride much smoother than our boat ever would." He went on to tell us if we were real serious about coot hunting, it would help if we painted more of these "shadows" on the sides of our craft. One last thing he made a point of telling us was to wear life preservers, and to tie a line from the guns to the boat.

With those precautions ringing in our ears, we headed to Alex's house to re-string our decoys, as we remembered the condition in which we'd found the rest of the rope in that shed.

I kiddingly told Alex's wife, "Chester said that we had to paint duck decoys on the sides of your boat."

There were so many sparks, you'd thought I'd kicked the fireplace log. She sputtered about how it had taken her hours to get that waterline straight, and we weren't about to touch it. (Doesn't everyone's wife tend to those little details?)

Stepping out of arms reach, I told her it was just a suggestion. Then I made the mistake of adding, "If you're really was opposed to the idea, maybe we can wait until we were sure the hunting is as good as we think it will be.

Deadly silence, accompanied by a pointing finger, directed me back out to the boat where Alex and I finished loading our gear.

The next day the wind wasn't blowing too hard, and that the two of us could sneak off from work, we trailered Alex's craft about five miles to a handy boat-ramp on the north side of Barnstable, and stuck her in the water. Flowing over the swells for a half mile along the shore, we headed for a spot we'd picked out earlier, by watching where the birds were sitting and diving for mussels.

About two hundred yards offshore, we threw the decoy anchors overboard, and marveled at how the nested 'coys slipped apart and strung themselves out.

Finally, we chugged over to our own appointed spot, threw the anchor out, killed the engine, and drifted down the slack of the line, rolling in the steady beat of the waves. As soon as the anchor fetched up, the boat swung around with a big heave into the wind. Eagerly, we loaded up our guns in a hurry, looking for action.

Much to our concern, the boat was riding into the breeze fine, but the bay's ground-swell was rolling under us 60 degrees off the wind. This resulted in a cross-sea that was both wet and nasty.

Well, here they came. With us sitting right out there in the middle of the 'coys, we felt as naked as a cake decoration at a bachelor's party, but the way those birds were coming at us you'd also think we'd sent out invitations.

Sea ducks don't fly in perfect V formations like puddle ducks, or geese. Instead, they look like a comic strip characterization of a swarm of bees. They fly with a big wad of them in the lead, all trying to be first, tapering off and stringing out to a trailing few.

A bunch of about thirty came racing each other into the confines of our spread. We swung up onto them and let a salvo fly.

Nothing happened! I mean, not a single feather came floating by!

Now Alex and I both were somewhat proud of our shooting eyes. To miss six times at thirty yards, raised four eyebrows.

Shortly afterwards, a couple more birds came by and we dropped them both, so we brushed aside that earlier episode, figuring we had been just a little over-eager.

The next flock that came was awesome. There's no other word for it. There were at least two hundred birds in the bunch.

Six shots echoed out over the water.

Not a feather!

We were sitting there staring at each other, with empty guns and open mouths. Meanwhile, the flight was so big that some of them were still over the 'coys, and in range.

What in the world was going on?

One problem we knew we had was the motion of the boat. It was throwing us all over the place. Enough so that we knew Chester's advice about life-vests and tying the guns down wasn't an idle remark. That problem not-withstanding, however, we knew we had a real hitch in our program.

About five flights later, the light slowly dawned. We had never in our lives shot at huge groups of birds like these. We weren't picking out individual ducks, we were just shooting into the bunches. Unconsciously, we must have felt we couldn't possibly miss with that many birds in the air.

Just maybe, we still had a couple of things to learn.

In the fall, the ocean takes on its winter hue. Gone are the friendly sparkles, the greens and blues, and the choppy, sassy little waves stirred by warm, southerly, summer breezes. In their place are white froth and somber tones of gray.

Storms, lugging their pent up misery way out at sea, send notice of their passage. Black ominous swells, having traveled hundreds of miles from these distant, horrendous gales, stretch as far as the eye can see.

The early winter wind, now a northerly, picks up a damp, dank bite that is straight out of the endless frozen nights of James

Bay, Canada, if it's a nor'wester; Greenland or Labrador, if a nor'easter. It chills to the bone, and the feeling one gets out on the water is of haunting loneliness.

We'd been there less than an hour, and I was toughing it out. My stomach was coming up to meet the back of my tongue with every swell. I was bruised from getting thrown around by the chop, frozen from the cutting wind, and I was wet through my oils from the spray. On top of that, I was almost out of shells, and I wanted to go home.

It was about then that Alex leaned over the gun'nel to pick up a bird that was drifting by, and stayed there, barking at the waves. Grabbing his coat-tail to keep him in the boat, I asked him if he had an opinion about duck-hunting on the open ocean. Not sharing my humor, he raised his green face and groaned something about leaving the decoys, then went back to his serenade.

Rolling him into the bottom of the boat so I could get at the outboard, I got us underway. I hauled the anchor, picked up one more bird we couldn't reach without the motor, and tried to retrieve our decoys. That's how I discovered there was no way to pick up a long string of 'coys in a stiff wind, and crossing sea.

Blue with the cold, green with the sea, I finally pulled the decoys until I came to their anchors, cut them free, and headed in. Thank the good Lord it was an onshore wind. I figured later on I'd go pick up the rigs, when they'd drifted onto the beach.

I rounded the jetty, and after the short run to the landing, got Alex loaded into his truck, the boat loaded onto the trailer, then we headed for home.

With my head hanging out the open window, I too began offloading ballast, and continued all the way back to our side of the Cape. We made it into Alex's yard, where we dry-heaved to a stop.

Alex's wife, with a smile on her face she didn't try to hide, called mine to come get what remained of me.

DANCING NAKED

While I waited, I tried to stuff into a garbage bag the five coot we'd gotten with our four boxes of shells.

Between the smell of the birds and the gas cans, along with what Alex had so indiscreetly left in the boat, my wife arrived before I could finish my self-imposed suffering. She loudly questioned my sanity and moral convictions, closed her eyes, and refused to come near me 'til I finished my task. Once finished, I crawled away--dragging the birds with me--from the scene of our calamity.

Somehow Alex had managed to get the guns into the house on his own. The two of us, in our weakened condition, with the earth feeling like it was still heaving under our bodies, tried to convince the girls they had to deliver the birds to Chester. Then we asked our loving (Or was that laughing?) spouses, to go over to the shore and try to find our hundred-dollar decoys, and drag them up into the dunes. We suggested they should be hidden, before our expensive investment was "misappropriated" by some sticky-fingered beach-comber. That would give us a day or two to get our strength back, so we could haul them home.

They didn't show much pity for our plight, but grudgingly agreed, figuring it to be the lesser of two-evils when compared to playing Florence Nightingale.

Being smarter than we, they convinced one of the neighbor's kids to come help them. Then, sputtering something about fools and their money, departed, leaving us in our misery to some welcome peace and quiet. We already knew it was going to be a long time before they'd let us forget this one.

It snowed that night, not that Alex or I gave a hoot. It's just that it gave our decoys a little more cover where the girls had hidden them, and guarantee the two of us a little more time before we absolutely had to get on our feet.

Anyone who's ever been sea-sick, and I mean real, real seasick, not just a little case of the queasies, knows what we were going through. We were down for two days before the two of us could finally navigate on our own, and a couple more before food took on much appeal.

Always helpful, Chester had sent his sympathy back with the girls, And said he'd warned us. "Should'a used a dory!" he told them. "At anchor, a dory cuts through the swells better, and doesn't thrash around in a chop, because it sits deeper in the water. A dory would have made a more stable gunning-platform too, and the chances are them-there boys wouldn't'a gotten sick."

The way the girls related this, it kept sounding like, "I told you so!"

The afternoon Chester called and asked if we were ready to try his stew, Alex and I took a pair of skis to the shore. It was another typical, gray, Cape Cod November day, with a blustery, onshore wind, and spitting snow.

Knowing there was no real choice we trudged on off down the beach and found the shadows right where the girls had placed them. Naturally, as part of the price for the directions we'd gotten from them, we also received a complete tale of horrendous effort, and hardship. Where have all the pioneer women gone?

We shook off the snow, untangled our pricey decoys, nested them properly, tied them down to the skis, then dragged them back the mile or so to the parking lot.

On the way home, we stopped by to accept Chester's invitation.

As we pulled up to the house, I noticed Harry sitting on the back door step. Not thinking too much of it at the time, we went up to the door and knocked. Being dog-lovers, we spoke to Harry much as we would a neighbor, said "Hello", and inquired of his health.

He got up, smiled at us, wagged his tail slowly, and stood

there expectantly with his nose to the door, so he could squeeze in ahead of us when it opened.

It was Chester's wife who came to the door. She was a little woman, as stooped and gray as Chester. She smiled, and nodded us in, exchanging pleasantries.

Harry, making sure he'd be first, started through the door, and froze dead in his tracks. Wheeling around, on, between, and under our feet, he let out a loud, "Whuff" and bolted back outside, almost knocking us down in the process.

Alex and I stood there, looking at Harry, wondering what had gotten into him. He in turn stood there on the lawn, looking back suspiciously, his ruff all raised and his wet nose working away like crazy.

That's when the smothering, completely-encompassing odor slammed into us. Almost indescribable, it appeared to be a mixture of broccoli, parsnip, cod-liver oil, and rotten skunk.

Then Chester appeared in the dark interior of the kitchen. Waving his arm and smiling away like a Cheshire cat, he hollered, "C'mon in boys! C'mon in! Don't pay no never-mind to that-there fool dog, c'mon in. Harry's just got hisself in a snit t'day. C'mon in."

Looking at one another, we stepped into their kitchen, a little reluctant to leave Harry's fresh air behind.

"Hey there boys, don't that-there stew smell 'bout as good as anythin' you ever smelt?"

Alex, starting to look a familiar shade of green again, stuttered and stammered a little, and said that it sure as heck did, and that we were sorry we weren't going to be able to join them for supper. It was "my" anniversary, he lied, and we had reservations at a big fancy restaurant where we were going to take the girls for a once-a-year celebration.

Chester sagged another inch or two. Looking crestfallen, he

replied that was a real shame. Settling into a chair, he told us how he'd "hung the birds proper" after he'd cleaned 'em. "Four or five days, 'til the feathers pulled out easy, so's they'd be tender." He rambled on, almost as if this were a continuation of our education in the ways to hunt coot proper.

"Then I plucked 'em real careful. Don't want to tear the skin, and maybe lose some of the fat."

He went on to say how he'd, "Singed the pinfeathers with one a' them-there gasoline blowtorches you boys dug outta my shed."

After the birds were ready, he and the missus "boiled 'em up in a big pot with some special herbs (he pronounced the "H") some celery and onions, and you know, got a good broth a'goin."

I remember how he leaned forward, whispering as if he were imparting an old family secret when he explained how he'd "tossed some root vegetables in the pot, like taters, and carrots, parsnips, turnips, and that kind'a stuff, whilst the ol' lady de-boned the birds. I had her stick the carcasses back in to keep the flavor a'buildin', but the meat would'a cooked to mash iffen that'd been left in the pot."

He "allowed" as how it was, "'bout reduced 'nough now, so's she can swap the meat with the bones, and it'll take up some of the seasoning whilst we let it rest a bit."

Chester's wife stood there all this time, wiping her hands, and wrapping them in her apron nervously. Looking a little sad, she appeared drawn-out from the day's effort. A wisp of hair that had somehow escaped her hair-net waved slowly in the air, moving with the motion of her head as she turned, looking from speaker to speaker. She seemed to be a little confused, and maybe three words behind the conversation.

I kicked Alex, and said, "You're crazy! That's tomorrow night, and I oughtta know, seeing as how it's 'my anniversary.'"

The sun picked that moment to come out, and the kitchen brightened a thousand-fold.

I could see Chester straighten up. The smile was back, though his eyes were still a little nervous, darting from one of us to the other. He wasn't sure if he dared get his hopes up for real, until he'd checked out our faces.

About this time his wife caught up with what we were saying. With a huge smile, she opened her arms, wrapping Alex and me into her stale, motherly embrace.

"You 'can' come to eat?" she beamed.

Ever feel at times like maybe there was an angel looking over your shoulder?

Not taking any more chances that Alex might come up with another excuse, I jumped right in and said, "Your darned right, Sarah! What time's supper?"

Alex sighed as he slumped behind the wheel of his truck, slamming the door after him.

I felt bad, but immediately began defending my actions.

"What else could we do, Alex? They had their hearts set on us coming to supper. Besides, if our wives ever heard about us supposedly taking them out to dinner for 'my anniversary', we'd have-to for sure. Probably out of our camp money to boot!"

Alex grudgingly agreed, and mumbled something about feeling seasick again. Then he brightened and suggested we bring a gift to the hostess. He said he knew, "just the wine to go with a meal like this."

I eyeballed him, not quite trusting the way he had made that statement.

He picked up on my expression. "No, no, I wouldn't do that," he said. "I know a good, strong, fruity wine that we might be able to wash the taste of coot down with, is all."

Arriving promptly at five o'clock, bottle in hand, (Do all old folks eat this early?), we said "Hi" to Harry, still holding his step down in the gathering darkness.

Not having learned his lesson yet, he scrambled up and pressed his nose against the door, ready to beat us into the warm kitchen. Having a better memory than Harry, Alex knocked on the door and stepped aside, while I waited out of harm's way, off the steps completely.

Chester came to the door, booming out his, "Hello, boys. C'mon in. Welcome."

The door swung open, and Harry sauntered in.

Alex and I exchanged looks, shrugged our shoulders, and followed him through the door.

The smell this time was of fresh-baked, yeast bread, and other goodies only hinted at. The kitchen was full of warmth from the oven, and these two old octogenarians, radiant with excitement at the thought of having company. They stood there side by side, Chester's arm around Sarah, beaming like two proud children.

The furniture was still the black-painted, rickety, old kitchen set, but there was a fresh table linen covering the red and white checked oil cloth. The table was set with what must have been wedding china that they probably hauled out from some dusty attic only on special occasions. Stemmed crystal goblets shone, and the silver was real.

I was truly stunned. I mentally thanked my thoughtful wife for insisting I bring along a little plant for "Chester's missus" as a more personal hostess gift than the bottle of wine we intended to share. It looked very pretty on the table between the candles.

They warmed to our heartfelt compliments like puppies to a pat.

We sat and shared conversation, wine, and companionship with our dinner. (This could no longer be referred to by the more common term, supper.) The bread was wonderful, the wine did chase the taste of coot out of our mouths, and the dessert was the best, chocolate, steamed pudding I had ever eaten.

After dawdling over coffee that was as rugged as the day's weather, we helped with the dishes in spite of their protests. Then, thanking them mightily for their hospitality, we patted Harry, and worked our way out the door.

Chester stepped out on the back step with us, and asked if we might be able to come by on "Saturday next", if we had the time. He said he had something he wanted to show us.

As I shook his hand one last time, to thank him again for a wonderful evening, I handed him another little bottle of "Rum-Runner" brandy".

Taking it, he held it up to the light shining through the open door.

He looked at me with a serious face and thanked me. He said he thought he'd save this bottle for some real special day, like the next time he, "sold a string of dee-coys for a hundred dollars." It was then, that I saw the twinkle in his eye.

Chester was puttering around his shed when we arrived on Saturday. He looked up and hollered, "C'mon in here boys. C'mon in!"

Leaves chased each other around the freshly mown field. We stepped out of the raw wind into Chester's own private domain.

He'd hung pictures on the walls, put a rug down, and found some old furniture. A pot-bellied stove he'd dug out of somewhere was cooking away in the middle of the room. Harry was happy. He was lying on a pile of blankets nearby, so comfortable in the glow that all he could do was smile at us, and thump his tail a couple of times.

There were a couple of chairs sitting next to the wall, surrounded by piles of shavings and some blocks of wood that were slowly turning into hand-carved boats. Chester explained that he'd fixed it up so that when his old buddies and their wives came by most every day, as he hoped they would, the menfolk could sit out here in the shed to whittle, and smoke their pipes whilst the women gossiped, and socialized in the house.

After discussing the weather and other small talk, he reached over behind an ancient shell-box and brought out two pair of the prettiest little Shelldrake decoys I'd ever seen.

Handing them to us, he said, "Boys, I been a'thinkin'. You kind'a got the short end of the stick with them-there shadows.

"Now, iffen you'll remember, I tol'ja when we started this-here project you could have anythin' else you found in here for the one price. Well now, when we was a'cleanin' out, we didn't make it up to the loft, did we?"

"Wantin' ta finish things off, I was a'pokin' 'round up there and came across these-here little birds.

"As I recollect, accordin' to that-there deal we shook hands on, I figure that they rightfully belong to you!"

Dumbfounded, I hugged that wonderful old goat, spun around on my heel, and bolted out of there before I cried, and embarrassed all of us more than I care to think about.

Well, that was a number of years ago now. Strangely, the urge to eat coot stew has never re-occurred, in spite of the fact not one iota of that adventure has ever faded from memory.

Since then, Chester, too, has passed on, but a pair of his Shelldrake 'coys are still sitting on my mantle, smiling at me and "Makin' sure I do things up-proper." And at times, when the light's just right, I could swear they too have a certain familiar twinkle in their eyes.

Full of warmth and good memories, I nod and smile back.

DANCING NAKED

DANCING NAKED

THE LIVING SEA

Carefully looking one views the sea
beauty and rhythm our senses perceive
wave upon wave roll close to my feet
as pebbles grind stone into sand
make a song most alluring.

A home without walls for elegant creatures
of soft cover and firm claw in harmony be
no thought of color or differences here.
All is not peaceful in this beautiful scene,
sorrow and pain are experienced by all,
as life passes through stages,
first birth, then love, and finally death.

Unacknowledged the stages press on,
not recognized by the lives they govern.
Pre-knowledge most wisely denied,
so awareness of pain is not known.

Up to the surface six legs do crawl,
oblivious to the bleached lacy tapestries
that rise and fall in broken strands
of delicate foaming art.

The wind rises with support of the moon,
to play music most pleasant.
Each line is new and never repeated,
bringing infinite joy to those who listen.
and comprehend this soft whisper of God.

DANCING NAKED

Surveying the vast scene unveils,
a peace resident memory knows not.
For this sound is broken by powerful storms
bringing danger to humans and
the work of their hands.

As a mother folds her children in her arms,
so the breaking waves enfold
young lives below the swell,
and bring comfort to fragile life.

Being the greatest part of Mother Earth,
the sea softly tells Father Moon,
"Fear not, all is in control my dear.
For underneath are the loving arms
of the One who created us all."

Oh mighty sea-tender sea
You are His for He made You,
and His breath formed the dry land.

Each day utters speech as
a tiny sparrow in her beach grass nest
loudly sings a triumphant benediction.
In the deep dark depths of the sea
small dolphins and might whales
resound hymns of hope and joy.

Their lives seem simple to intelligent men.
How tenderly these largest animals of all
emulate our common emotions,
to feed and teach and love their young.

DANCING NAKED

To all life on earth and seas
just one charge is given:
Follow ancient directions
to love and obey God the Creator,
and to prosper their children
with tender loving care.

Oh seas, what wonderful lessons you teach,
and examples you show.
If only mankind would learn from you.

DANCING NAKED

DANCING NAKED

MENDING NETS

Over and under, back through the loop.
   Pull the line tight to anchor the knot.
On to the next hole the shuttle he pushes,
   stretching his arms,
   repeating the task.

"Ho," he shouts to his friend
   sitting across the weathered dock.
No need to look, just knowing he's there,
   deep breaths of warm salt air.

Lifting loud voices they begin to sing
   sea chanties, work songs or even
   praises to the women they've known.
Ditties they cast to the winds and are gone,
   folk songs they voice from a hundred
   year span.

Memories of days far out on the sea
   pulling lines with hardened hands
   while dreaming of soft touches
   back home on the sand.
Crude men these singing off key
   with visions of loved ones
   gently sipping their tea.

Now back to the nets their interest is known
   tomorrow's catch may all be lost
   by an uneven hitch
Captain and crew careless work they will eschew.

DANCING NAKED

DANCING NAKED

ANGELIC INTERVENTION

Jacob is a good boy, with looks and charm that endear him to relatives and friends alike. Reports from school reflect his diligence, work ethic, and honesty. The only weakness seems to be that he doesn't follow instructions exactly. For example; a homework assignment given to his class was to write a one-page overview of the advantages and disadvantages of using pesticides on vegetable gardens. Jacob studied, wrote and turned in a paper he called, "Detoxifying Worms To Protect the Food Of Robins." Oblique? The teacher thinks so and asks him to do it over.

Jacob's parents both have good jobs in the business world. His two sisters, older by two and four years, participate in the usual after school programs most young girls take: dance class, swimming lessons, softball, etc. These things keep the girls busy, and they find it easy to ignore Jacob. No matter, being their youngest, the parents patronize him, and accede to almost every request he makes as long as it's safe and uplifting.

One day Father comes home from work, and his face is lit up with smiles. Just in time for supper, the family gathers, and unable to contain himself any longer, he announces, "Guess what? My request for vacation has been approved. We're going to have off the last two weeks of summer, before school starts again."

They may have eaten, but no one would remember what. Everyone was talking at once, and it took a few minutes for Mother to steer them into a discussion of where they should go. Disney World and Six Flags were ruled out, as too expensive, and besides, they'd already been there more than once. Remembering trips of her own, when she was young, Mother suggested the coast of Maine might be just what they needed. Lots of fresh air, sunshine, and yummy places to eat, and explore.

Sitting there, enjoying the Buzz his announcement had started, Father mentions, "In those two weeks, the water temperature in Maine is the year's warmest, but the air can have a bite to it, especially at night."

Come morning, Mother telephoned the Maine Chamber Of Commerce to request information. A few days later, an avalanche of mail began to arrive. Maps of Maine, and hundreds of brochures listing rental cottages, Bed and Breakfasts, hotels, restaurants, historic places to visit, houses of worship, museums, hiking trails, sight-seeing cruises and more. For weeks, the house was strewn with brochures, letters, and testaments, telling the glory of particular vacation spots.

Getting close to decision time, Mother gathered us together and asked, "Do we want to rent a three or four-bedroom cottage? Can it be on, or near the water?"

"If we're bringing beach umbrellas, toys and coolers, we don't want to have to drive the car to the ocean, "Replies the older sister."

"That's right," says the second sister. "We want to be able to walk right from the cottage to the water's edge, but can we get one with Wi-Fi too?"

"I don't think your father will agree to that," says Mother, "but you've got to help me go through all these brochures to find out what's available, and what we can afford."

Most of the day, and a few hours of the next were spent on the computer, and telephone.

The weeks rushed by, with everyone gathering clothes and

supplies; the camera, hiking boots, sneakers, binoculars, books, games to play in the car and more.

The day before we left, Father stared at the pile on the living room floor, and announced, "Hey guys, we can't take the whole house with us, just what we need for two weeks!"

Everything had been positioned, so packing the SUV wouldn't be a problem . . . it was anyway. There's something about packing a car that creates chaos, but it gets done. Finally, we all piled in. Windows down, the radio blasting, we were on our way.

Getting started, Father drives, Mother sits beside him, and the three siblings share the bench seat in the back, with feet tangled over backpacks and duffel bags. The trip is looong and boooring. They stop for lunch at a fast-food joint for burgers, followed by ice cream cones. At last, they drive across the causeway from the mainland to the barrier island where the cottage is located. Father parks the car in front of a real estate office.

Jacob and his sisters climb out to stretch their legs, while Father and Mother receive directions, a key and tips on using the cottage appliances. It's just a short distance to the gray cedar-shake cottage that will be the family home for the next 12 days. Running to the porch, while Mother unlocks the door, the children scramble inside and lay claim to their bedrooms.

"This one is mine"

"No, that one is yours," the girls shout excitedly.

As usual, Jacob gets the smallest room, but it has a window facing east. "This will be great," he says. "I can watch the sun come up from my bed."

Mother examines the kitchen sink, stove and refrigerator. "These appliances are much older than ours at home, but they bring back memories of by-gone days, and my childhood," She says to Father.

"Well," Says Father with a smirk, "At least we have indoor plumbing."

Father unpacks the SUV and the children haul their own luggage into their selected bedrooms. As Father and Mother complete the unpacking, the children run to the immense rocks lining the water's edge. Jacob looks out to sea and takes long deep breaths of salt air. The girls are fascinated watching the antics of seagulls, and they scurry carefully across the rocks.

In the following days the family hikes trails at Acadia National Park, tours a light house, walks the seashore kicking their feet in the surf, swims in the community pool, and learn maritime history at a museum. With all of this activity there is still plenty of time to lounge on the rocks and read. Of course there are expeditions to local restaurants to savor old favorite family seafood, such as boiled lobster and fried clams.

At the first restaurant while all are reading the menu, Father says, "Let's make this a learning experience with each of us reaching outside the envelope to order an entree they have never eaten before; muscles Kiev, calamari, king crab legs, escargot, or what ever catches your fancy."

"That's quite a challenge," Says Mother. As the food is tasted, there are some raised eyebrows and far more smiles around the table.

One afternoon Jacob is a little exuberant playing and running in a nearby field. He bumps his sisters so hard, they all go sprawling in the sandy grass. "Ouch, watch where you're going," the girls howl. With skinned elbows, and one twisted wrist, they stand up and pick leaves, straw, and sundried seaweed off their clothes .

Mother comes to the rescue, dresses their wounds and questions the cause of their tumble.

She calls loudly, "Jacob, come in here immediately."

Jacob is scolded intently about respecting others, and personal safety. Grabbing his jacket he walks out and sits on the cottage steps to pout. He hardly eats any supper, then returns to the steps. Still mad, after a while he decides to go for a walk, without telling the family.

The barrier island where the cottage is located joins the mainland by a road over the causeway, and also by a footbridge. Walking over that bridge is a bit challenging. It's old and weathered, long and shaky. On a good day it takes a person 10 minutes to walk all the way across. The bridge is 20 feet above the water, and the water is 40 feet deep. This is a favorite place for local fisherman to catch lobsters. This day, a single lobster boat is working up stream of the bridge. It's quite a picturesque view.

At the footbridge Jacob rests his elbows on the rail, and looks at the bright lights and hears the music over on the mainland. He says to himself, "It seems like everyone is having a good time over there. I deserve some fun too, and I'd sure like to join in. I'll show my family that I don't need them to have a good time."

Looking around to see that no one is watching, he begins to walk across. Jacob remembers Father's words that it can be cold at night in Maine at this time of year. He draws his jacket tightly around himself and digs in the pockets for a pair of gloves. Not wanting to miss the fun he can already see, he hops, skips and jumps along.

The old bridge creaks and groans. Before reaching the middle of the bridge, he hears cracking noises, and Jacob breaks through the floor-boards, crashing all the way down into the water.

Surprised, and scared, he tries to swim up to the surface. He is a good swimmer in a bathing suit, but wearing street cloths and a heavy jacket he flounders, and sinks to the bottom.

Remembering his swim lessons, he opens his eyes under water but the water is murky and he sees hardly anything. By flapping his arms he rises to the surface, only to be struck by a wave and sent back to the bottom. Out of breath, now he panics. He works feverishly to regain the surface, gasping and thrashing there to stay afloat before he sinks again for the third time. He's light-headed and feels like he is drifting out of consciousness, like he wants to go to sleep.

Over to his left there is a diver in a bright white suit, and another on the right side. Together they reach under Jacob's arms and drag him to the surface. They set him on one of the bridge pylons where he coughs and catches his breath. Both divers, still shining white, try to get Jacob to talk, and ask if he will be alright. He manages to grunt and nod his head. Immediately the divers disappear from Jacob's sight without so much as a splash. Confused, Jacob thinks about his rescuers, and wonders who they were. "Could they have been angels?" He muses foggily. "That's the only thing that makes sense, or does it?"

About this time the lobster boat comes along-side, and the fishermen lift Jacob into their boat. Revving the engine they head to shore. The noise is too loud to talk, so they know not to ask any questions. They wrap Jacob in a blanket, and one man puts his arms around him to keep him warm. The fisherman help Jacob out of the boat, and carry him up the bank.

By this time it's dusk, and a crowd of people watch from the bridge and the shore. Called by some of the townspeople, Father and Mother rush down the bank and hug Jacob. When he is able to speak, Jacob tells everyone how he was rescued by two shining white divers.

The fishermen scratch their heads and say, "There was no dive boat, or dive flags there, no reason for divers to be there at all. What did they look like?"

"Well, they had no flippers, air tanks or face masks. Their suits were so bright that I couldn't tell if they were wearing wet suits or not," Answers Jacob.

The people watching begin to ask each other, "No one else was out there. Could it be that he was rescued by angelic beings?"

Two paramedics carry him to an ambulance, and take him to the hospital to be treated for hypothermia. Jacob's parents hurry into the hospital room to be with him, and receive the doctor's report. His condition seems to be mild, but the hospital keeps him overnight to track his vital signs.

Jacob repeats his rescue narrative time and again, always word-for-word, always mentioning his angelic rescuers.

Reporters from the local newspaper interview Jacob. They love the story. The senior reporter asks, jokingly, "Well, did you wrestle with the angels? Is your hip out of joint?"

Jacob doesn't appreciate this ridiculous question and answers, "Of course not. Don't be silly."

The reporters hurry back to the office to search the archives for evidence of similar incidents of angelic rescues in the past. They find many rescue articles, but none involving angels.

As they work, the cub reporter asks, "What were all those questions about wrestling and hip joints?"

His partner stops work and answers, "It's about the Bible story in Genesis. You remember, don't you, how Jacob wrestled all night with an angel? In the morning the angel saw that he could not overpower Jacob, so he wrenched his hip just by touching Jacob's hip socket."

The next day the local newspaper runs a banner story about two angels rescuing a drowning boy.

Jacob is never the same after that vacation. He is kinder, more gentle and never pesters his sisters. He even follows his teacher's requests for homework. If you ask him about his Maine vacation he says simply, "I fell through an old footbridge into the ocean and was rescued by two angels."

Do you believe in angels? Jacob and his family do with certainty.

DANCING NAKED

FIELDS/ the girl in the window

The lot looks like it had been bombed out. Gray, potholed, warn, withered, dying, remnants of old dead, half-buried branches, rain-soaked and dried scraps of old papers, newspapers blurred of past dates, windblown, caught and tangled. Woodchucks have made this field a raucous tunneling playground.

   I watched nearby with memories of sweet days of long ago summers. There was a meadow just before the copse where rats, skunks and rabbits ruled the area.

   Neighborhood kids played baseball, hide and go seek and tag in and among the overgrown bushes. Old warn, torn baseballs, broken kites, tangled strings. Scaring each other, they pinged hardened dried berries at one another, claiming they were only the ever-annoying grasshoppers, tangling in each others' hair, attacking them all as they screamed in fake fearful scary delight. When the day was over, time to head on home, we picked burrs from each others' hair and clothes, giggling all the while.

   Nearby and abutting farmers kept fences dug deep into the ground to keep the burrowing rodents and creatures out and away from their precious fields of fertile rows.

   The men who came later to clear, reclaim and restore those fields were from the homeless shelter, working for food and regular daily schedules . . . a purpose where they had had none previously, or at least not in the more recent past. They were enrolled in this farming program to make a life for themselves that was better than their last. Perhaps family lost, perhaps neighborhood influences, drink, drugs, loss, depression, gangs, loss, loss, loss. All pushed, pulled into pockets of an unforgiving abyss. Decimated, dissolved into a past.

Some were young, with hopes of change. Others were older needing personal guidance daily to keep their eyes toward a new and yet uncertain fruitful goal. No women. I suppose any women would have swayed them, lured them toward un-self-saving and the temporary cul de sac of emptiness. For they'd have no self assuredness that would offer them a suredness to do the best for themselves . . . at least, better.

When I was a little girl, so much younger, I watched from my bedroom window to see how the fields of green grew, changed, evolved, took over that barren lot. The trash was trucked away, the wild grasses piled into heaps for compost. The soil was tilled to fluff, divided and planted in geometric rows. Rich earth that soon supported so many greens, some large and leafy, some tall and delicate.

They came in a long white van early in the morning, every morning, scattered all throughout the fields, accomplishing a lot before the heat of the day. One tall man in uniform stood by, directing the crew. Daily, the directed men separated into twos, walked the rows, planting and replanting individual seeds, carefully measuring spaces between. Always the same men.

My mother knew my curious interest, told me to never go down to see them, not to talk with them. Ever. Not even to wave, she said, although I knew, was aware, that they looked up at me looking down on them from my third floor bedroom window while they sat drinking with each other and wiping their foreheads during breaks. Our secret.

Their drink was measured from a large metal cask that looked like it may have kept the liquid chilled. Refreshing, cool, lovely.

Poured sometimes, sprayed on one another for relief. Some just lay there, sore, strong, muscular arms across their bellies, fingers knotted together with their hats or scarves pulled down over their faces while they slept. Others would lie face down, the backs of their shirts, sweaty and soaked, often reaching up to swat any insect or whatever that lit or crawled over them. Some even pulled out books and lay in the grass to read.

When my mother called me into the big yellow kitchen for dinner, she had to call once, twice and sometimes three times for me to pull myself away. Dreams. Ribbed grains, corn, popcorn stitch cabbages and smaller, delicate french knots of lettuces. Bright twists of peppers, hidden red tomatoes, long-tailed cucumbers. Frilly fringed carrot stems. And I watched them, watched them for years, watched them as they knit their field into a beautiful blanket of green, patterns I wished I could knit for myself.

"What takes you so long to come?" she nattered at me, with rote interest and little enthusiasm.

I could hardly squeak out, "Nothing." But it was something.

She worried that it was the men I watched, the men taking me away into a frighteningly unhealthy direction.

Her daughter, for whom she herself had dreams.

I saw intricate stitches in the brussell sprouts, wild curvy cables in the corn stocks, manifesting gorgeous yellow fringes for their tops. Intricately delicate patterns in the flowery borders. All lovely.

The bees buzzed crazily, dizzily, happily, fruitfully, with renewed energy in that once fallow field. I watched.

But she was right.

I ran indoors from camp, from play, always timing myself to see what was happening in that field, to catch up on what I may have missed.

She knew.

As I grew older, it was always the men. Yes. And soon it became just one man.

Did he know that I was his spy? A daily viewing of curiosity, emblematic of thread and yarn and novels. It never seemed to change. Our secret.

One especially who always stopped to avidly read instead of taking his lunch. And through my binoculars, spy glass, I could see that his books changed. Almost daily. He seemed to eat them up. I was more and more curious. New titles, new interest. The fact that he looked up at me, the fact that he surreptitiously waved, (hidden from the director) the fact that he smiled when doing so, touched himself.

Over the field. I worried about slipping downstairs to meet with him, but the director was at his back. My mother was at mine. I planned. But it was not to be.

What was so interesting about the books he seemed to be gobbling up? He held them up to me, one at a time, always smiling. each day something new. I looked for their titles.

'Peyton Place.'

Another day: 'Lolita.'

And then: 'Tropic of Cancer.'

'Portnoy's Complaint.'

I was getting the point.

'Valley of the Dolls.'

Chills.

I pulled back, convincing myself not to look again. This was not simple anymore. Oh yeah, I stopped. But only for a while.

And then one day he was not there. Nor the next.

I waited. Curious, foolishly still longing. He was gone.

Time passed. It took a while for me to realize it, but I finally did. My Ma was right.

The men became just men, nobody in particular, nobody looking back at me, just men, working men, troubled men.

More time passed.
Never again was he there.
My summer years.
I realized my innocence.
My interest drew me back into my bedroom, sitting alone, where I knitted a warm, tufted, fringed and glorified blanket of soft green variegated wool, imitating those summer fields nearby.

Soon there were no men. I grew, went off to college.

And now I return. The fields are once again deserted, empty, unplowed, unkempt. A wild destruction.

I curl myself into my own knitted green field, peppered with gloriously embroidered secret dreamy memories, warm in my bed, and remember.

DANCING NAKED

DANCING NAKED

A MOTHER'S GIFT

Once a week
    Call and chat.
Once a day
    Think of me.

Every minute
    Of every hour
    Of every day
Know.

DANCING NAKED

DANCING NAKED

EMILY

This poem was written about a cat named Emily who had been abandoned and been in our animal shelter for several months. Nearing Christmas, most of the other kittens had been adopted out, but Emily was an older cat, not as popular as kittens.

Dear Santa:
All I want for Christmas
Is a family of my own,
Santa, would you please find one,
To take me to their home?
I've been good, so very good,
I think you will agree.
I won't ask for very much,
A girl to play with me.

I'd like to hide and watch them all,
From underneath their tree,
Waiting 'til the very end,
How quiet I will be.
She'll open all her lovely gifts,
Each wrapped with bow and name,
She'll laugh and giggle with each one,

DANCING NAKED

A toy, a book, a game.

But when she's done, and thinks that's all,
The gifts there are to be,
She'll look around in case there's one,
She may have missed, you see,
She'll search the room, look high and low,
No new gifts to be found,
"The tree!" she'll say, "Let's look in there,"
"You don't suppose there'll be,
Another gift, an extra gift just 'specially for me?"

Down on her hands and knees she'll creep,
Under the boughs to see,
If there is only one more gift,
To finally find me!

Surprise! She sees my fur and tail,
My eyes shining with love,
She'll pat my coat,
(It's black and white)
What a surprise I'll be!

I do love kids and other cats,
I'm a sweet and gentle girl,
This is my wish, my only wish,
Oh! Please give it a whirl,
Thank you, Santa, I will wait,
I do believe in you,
I know that you will grant my wish,

DANCING NAKED

That wishes do come true,
Find me a forever home,
And in it may there be,
A family of my very own,
A child to play with me!

Thank you,

Emily, the cat.

DANCING NAKED

# DANCING NAKED

ABOUT THE WRITERS

SHARON D. ANDERSON, PhD, RMT

S.D. Anderson is an Indie Author/Publisher, dedicated to her craft for more than 30 years. Writing in her genre, Visionary Fiction and Non-Fiction, all of her books, websites and blogs merge a far-seeing perspective of New Age and Ancient Wisdom from Eastern, Western, and Primordial Philosophies.
Living on her beloved Cape Cod, she actively participates in a weekly writers group through the Cape Cod Writers Center.
Here is the link to her Amazon Authors Page:
https://www.amazon.com/author/andersonsharon

Her Good Reads Author Page:
htttps://www.goodreads.com/angelicomm

DANCING NAKED

ROBERT BUYER

Robert Buyer was employed as an industrial technical writer for over 40 years. On retirement, he and his wife moved to Cape Cod where they serve their local church and Bob writes children's books and devotional meditations. Together the couple have raised three children and have led many church youth groups. They have fond memories of their three grown children from when they were young. The Buyers find Cape Cod to be excellent for watching and identifying wild sea birds.

Children today are barraged in every media with fantasy stories of inter-galactic travel, thinking machines programmed to do destruction and mass killings. These inputs may stretch children's imaginations but they harm the integrity of their thought patterns. Contrarily, children's books that I write depict animals and people living on earth and sharing their joys and sorrows. The main characters in these stories show love and faith while quietly demonstrating peaceful, intelligent actions. Reading my books give children confidence (knowing that they are special and very loved) and compassion. (righting wrongs in peaceful ways)

My children's books bring hope and happiness to readers. Learning is also a goal of my books- they not only tell interesting stories, but they also help readers to learn new words, through a glossary, expand their understanding with questions to promote discussion, and usually contain a simple hands-on craft project.

These books do not teach religion. They advocate good will and prayer through the examples of the main characters.

DANCING NAKED

ARTHUR F. CLARK

We've all heard the old saw about being older than dirt. Well, there are days when I feel older than the dust they make dirt out of. The good years, when the memories I mine were first formed.

I walked on the decks of ships wrecked during the 1860's, before the "save the environment" movements cleaned the marshes. Those ships became part of my historical novel, "Until He Died", written to describe the end of the sailing era in the 1870's.

Civil War Veterans attended Memorial Day services in my youth. I knew their children and grandchildren, hence the Civil War Trilogy I'm just finishing. If you think that's far-fetched, I'm talking sixty-five years after that war ended. How many veterans do you know from WWII, which ended Seventy years ago?

In the thirties, I was an eye-witness to the German Zeppelins, Hindenburg, and Graf Zeppelin, making their regularly scheduled flights across Cape Cod, on the way to a docking site in New Jersey. This inspired my historical novel, "Sea Smoke, and Low Tide" based on the craziness during the prohibition era of the 1920's and 30's.

A shorter novel about life on the Cape during the mid-40's is a coming of age story, and the pain suffered here at home during the war years. "Death and Summer Nights" is painfully nostalgic.

Then there's "Derelict", a man lost to alcohol, and the sea.

After five years of college and a stint in the Army, with the 77th Special Forces Group, I wrote the short story, "Bloodlines", found here, along with "Sitting Ducks", another nostalgia piece. The well is far from empty.

DANCING NAKED

TOBY ELLEN KALMAN

Toby grew up in a home where the Arts were most important. With her dad, she took life classes before she was ten years old. Then she painted walls and murals, inside and out at home and in her neighborhood. She is known to donate creative posters and sculptures to varied events such as businesses and fund-raisers.

Her dad's murals were later featured on TV's "Chronicle."

She attended the Museum School of Fine arts, Boston and University of Massachusetts, Amherst. As an artist, she has won awards, has worked in many different and varied media: sculpture, painting, structural building design, knitting, needlepoint painting, jewelry . . . and now writing where she continues to see and hear things that most people are not aware of.

She went on to lead adults who provide home day care for preschool children with creative exercises and cultural safety. Her leading creativity brought an expansion of brilliance and joy to each facility.

As a critic, she helps mould other people's ideas into a freshness that she strives for in her own work.

Her vivid mind is never at rest, drawing images and events outside of reality, as Jo-Henry, her fifteen foot tall gentle heroine in her short story, Jo-Henry's Day.

She currently lives happily in a home that she designed from structurally found bits and pieces of assorted restorative materials.

DANCING NAKED

GERI RIDER

As a reverse snow bird, Geri enjoys the beauty and serenity of the winter Cape and summers in Door County, Wisconsin. She is currently editing an anthology of short stories centered in the Midwest. She is happiest with sand between her toes and the sound of waves lapping at the shore. When it's pointed out that most people summer on the Cape, her standard answer is 'Have you ever experienced a Wisconsin winter?'

DANCING NAKED

DWIGHT RITTER

I am a writer and graphic designer. I see excitement in spaces where most people see only voids. I hear music in my head that has long since stopped. I cry secretly at certain tv commercials and wonder what God's plan is for me.

My mother was a concert pianist. . . a child prodigy from Massachusetts. In 1919 the Boston Herald referred to her as, "a nine year old pianist extraordinaire." She, too, heard music that others didn't. She, too, wept at Pepsi commercials.

My father studied art and wrote love letters to Mom. . .letters that would have captured the heart of any woman. Sadly, though, that was during the depression and he was raised to reach for the golden ring, so he went to medical school to provide an "honest living" for his family. He forgot how to cry. He no longer heard the music. His paintbrush went dry.

So it was clear that someone in my family was going to catch the disease called creativitusstupiditus.

It was me.

I went to a traditional museum school of art, followed by a Big Ten University. Dad talked to me about the golden ring but my heart kept hearing and feeling the sounds that Mom heard.

I married an artist (www.joannritterfineart) and began working in advertising, the only place where I could scratch people who didn't itch. I wrote ads, instructional booklets, television commercials. Also designed ads, trade show booths and set designs. Even wrote a few tv jingles and songs for Sesame Street. While I was working I wrote, filmed and edited, "Being

Amish." It was picked up by PBS and distributed for many years. After moving to Boston I started my own business providing creative services to companies. But like my father I felt compelled to chase the golden ring, sacrificing tummy bubbles and chills for a steady income. Oh me!

    Several years ago I resumed the goose bumps of lost music, resurrected the grace of a curved line, thawed the hardness of my creativity and put my life in the hands of a power far bigger than anything I had ever imagined. Quietly.

    I love to fly fish. The rhythm and grace of the process is beautiful. Delicate, soft and lethal. I've fished many waters in many countries. . .salt, fresh and murky. Caught some beautiful fish, so many that I don't need to lie about it.

    Several years ago I was given the opportunity to volunteer my time as a translator on medical mission trips to Guatemala, Nicaragua and Cuba. This has evolved into functioning as a surgical nurses assistant while translating. Operation Walk provides

    I also build cars. . .hot rods, those gleaming relics slammed close to the ground that growl and roar. I have a 1936 Ford Cabriolet and a 1940 Ford Pick Up.

DANCING NAKED

WADE SAYER

I was born and raised on Long Island, in a suburb of New York. My Mom stayed at home, my Dad commuted by Long Island Railroad to the city every day. I grew up in a post World War II, pre-TV, early transistor radio society. If we wanted to play, we went down the street to see our friends. We rode bikes, played in empty fields, woods and hung out at the candy store.

Summers were spent at the shore, swimming, sailing, fishing and crabbing; there were girls there too, but no one knew what to do. We had picnics, went on adventures, and mostly learned how to be kids.

In high school I played football, basketball and pitched on the baseball team. I never thought much about writing, until one teacher called me in front of the class, and to my great embarrassment, had me read my story. She told me that I had potential, and I believed her. I kept writing, thinking about writing and working at it after that.

Bouncing around after a couple misplaced years at college, I joined the Army and was sent to the Defense Language Institute in California. After learning a year's worth of Vietnamese, the Army assigned me to the 101st Airborne Division and0 off to Vietnam. I considered my options at the time, but decided to go in order to find out what life was actually like in a war zone, as a soldier. Surely, it wouldn't be like those dumb movies.

I finished college after the army, and then graduate school too. I started a career, and a family. And writing got pushed to the side. And while I wrote a couple of national studies and books in my career, I never really got back to it until I retired from my career.

Now, finally I am a writer. Novels, short stories and even poems. Sometime about military experiences, sometimes just life.

DANCING NAKED

MIKE TEMPESTA

My passion for music began with the Beatles. I remember standing in a record store called Discland in Waltham, Mass., and hearing "I Wanna Hold Your Hand" for the first time. I was mesmerized. And completely hooked; music is still in my fiber today. As a result, music is in my writing. I recently finished my eighth short story that is inspired by a song.

My writing began in high school. I took a journalism course because my dream was to be a sportswriter. The teacher, Helen Smith, told me I was good at it and no one had told me I was good at anything before.

So why not major in journalism at college? At Northeastern University, the only thing I applied myself to (in addition to frequenting the pub across the street) was the college newspaper.

I also began writing poems in college, thanks to a professor and poet named Joseph DeRoche.

After graduation I got my dream job: sportswriter at a large daily newspaper, the Middlesex News in Framingham. Next came the job as news editor at the Marlboro Enterprise followed by a job at the Pulitzer Prize winning Eagle-Tribune in Lawrence, where I was news editor then, columnist.

My newspaper career ended in 1998. I moved to Falmouth, wrote freelance articles, poetry, essays and began to write fiction. Seven years ago I self-published a novel, <u>Valentino's Opera</u>, about a Cape Cod lawyer who is consumed by alcoholism, begins to live a spiritual life through the 12 Steps, recovers and meets his true love.

These days I still write essays, fiction and poetry. The poems begin on my daily pre-dawn runs along the ocean road in Falmouth. I have run 20 marathons, including eight Boston

DANCING NAKED

Marathons, but those 26.2-mile odysseys are behind me. I run now because never do I feel more alive – save for catching a trout with my fly rod or a striped bass from my boat.

The best part of life at age 58 is the time I spend with my beloved Susan. We share passions for fishing, cooking, gardening and spirituality. And, of course, music.

DANCING NAKED